永恆的莎士比亞改寫劇本 ⑩

第十二夜

TWELFTH NIGHT

William Shakespeare ◆ 著

Emily Hutchinson ◆ 改寫 │ 蘇瑞琴 ◆ 譯

MP3

永恆的莎士比亞改寫劇本 ❿

第十二夜

TWELFTH NIGHT

作　　者	William Shakespeare, Emily Hutchinson
翻　　譯	蘇瑞琴
編　　輯	Gina Wang
校　　對	丁宥榆
內文排版	林書玉
封面設計	林書玉
製程管理	洪巧玲
出 版 者	寂天文化事業股份有限公司
電　　話	+886-(0)2-2365-9739
傳　　真	+886-(0)2-2365-9835
網　　址	www.icosmos.com.tw
讀者服務	onlineservice@icosmos.com.tw
出版日期	2016 年 10 月 初版一刷

版權所有 請勿翻印
郵撥帳號 1998620-0 寂天文化事業股份有限公司
劃撥金額 600（含）元以上者，郵資免費。
訂購金額 600 元以下者，加收 65 元運費。
〔若有破損，請寄回更換，謝謝〕

國家圖書館出版品預行編目 (CIP) 資料

永恆的莎士比亞改寫劇本 .10：第十二夜 / William
Shakespeare, Emily Hutchinson 作
；蘇瑞琴譯 .-- 初版 .-- [臺北市]：寂天文化，
2016.10
　面； 公分
ISBN 978-986-318-512-3(平裝附光碟片)
　873.43346　　　　　　　　　　　105018866

Contents

Background

Orsino, Duke of Illyria, loves the Countess
Olivia—but she will have nothing to do with him.
Orsino sends his page Cesario (the disguised Viola,
who has fallen in love with him) to plead his cause.
Olivia falls in love with Cesario.

Viola's twin brother Sebastian (whom she believes
has drowned in a shipwreck) arrives in Illyria.
Olivia mistakes Sebastian for his disguised sister,
and Sebastian falls in love with Olivia. More
complications follow before identities are revealed
and the story is brought to a happy end.

Cast of Characters

ORSINO: Duke of Illyria

SEBASTIAN: a young gentleman, Viola's brother

ANTONIO: a sea captain, friend of Sebastian

A SEA CAPTAIN: friend of Viola

VALENTINE and **CURIO:** gentlemen

SIR TOBY BELCH: Olivia's uncle

SIR ANDREW AGUECHEEK: Sir Toby's friend

OLIVIA: a rich countess

VIOLA: Sebastian's sister; later disguised as Cesario

MARIA: Olivia's gentlewoman in waiting

MALVOLIO: Olivia's steward

FABIAN: Olivia's servant

FESTE: Olivia's jester

LORDS, A PRIEST, SAILORS, OFFICERS, MUSICIANS, and **OTHERS**

ACT 1

Summary

伊利里亞公爵奧西諾對奧麗維婭一片癡情。薇奧拉從船難中被救起,來到伊利里亞,這場船難可能奪走她孿生兄長西巴斯辛的命。為了生計,薇奧拉易裝成男子,去公爵府上擔任差使。薇奧拉迅速地成為公爵最喜愛的僕役,並被差遣至奧麗維婭家替奧西諾公爵示愛。

同時,在美麗貴族奧麗維婭府上,她叔父托比‧培爾契爵士帶安德魯‧艾古契克爵士(培爾契爵士的酒肉朋友)前來,讓他贏得姪女的芳心。瑪利婭是奧麗維婭的貼身侍女,發現艾古契克爵士是個愚蠢的人,加入托比的行列,吹捧安德魯爵士,使他成為笑柄,但奧麗維婭對這些醉鬼的胡言亂語一點都不感到幽默。費斯特是奧麗維婭的弄臣,講笑話逗奧麗維婭開心。同時,古板的管家馬伏里奧對費斯特冒昧的幽默起了反感。

瑪利婭宣布奧麗維婭家門口有訪客光臨,但她拒絕接見任何人,直到馬伏里奧告訴她西薩里奧十分英俊才改變心意。奧麗維婭告訴西薩里奧,她永遠都不會愛上奧西諾公爵。奧麗維婭被西薩里奧所吸引,她差派馬伏里奧去找西薩里奧,給他一枚戒指,並推說戒指是西薩里奧留下來忘記帶走的。

Scene 1

An apartment in the duke's palace in Illyria. The **duke, Curio,** and **lords** enter. Musicians play.

DUKE: If music be the food of love, play on,
  Give me too much of it. By gorging,
  The appetite may sicken and so die.
  (Listening briefly) Enough! No more!
  It's not as sweet now as it was before.
  Oh, spirit of love! How alive and fresh you are!
  In spite of being as deep as the sea,
  Nothing precious comes to you without
  Losing some of its value even in a minute!
  Love has such variety that nothing can
  Equal its extravagance.

CURIO: Will you go hunt, my lord?

DUKE: Hunt what, Curio?

CURIO: The hart.

DUKE *(placing his hand on his heart)*: Why,
  That is what I'm doing. When my eyes first
  Saw Olivia, I thought she purified the air.
  That instant I was turned into a hart,
  And my desires, like fierce and cruel hounds,
  Have chased me ever since.

7

(**Valentine** enters.)

DUKE: Well? What news from her?

VALENTINE: My lord, I was not invited in.
Through her maid, the answer is this:
For seven summers, not even the sun
Will see her face. Like a nun, she will wear
A veil, weeping salt tears around her room,
To honor her dead brother's love, which
She wishes to keep fresh in sad memory.

DUKE: Oh, she who has such a tender heart
To pay this debt of love for a mere brother!
How will she love when Cupid's arrow
Strikes her heart?
Lead the way to sweet beds of flowers!
Love thoughts are richer under the bowers.

(**All** exit.)

Scene 2

The seacoast. **Viola, captain,** and **sailors** enter.

VIOLA: What country is this, friends?

CAPTAIN: This is Illyria, lady.

VIOLA: What am I doing in Illyria?
My brother is in heaven. But maybe
He is not drowned. What do you think?

CAPTAIN: Luckily, you yourself were saved.

VIOLA: Oh, my poor brother!
Maybe he was saved, too.

CAPTAIN: True, madam. After our ship split,
When we were clinging to the drifting boat,
I saw your brother tie himself to a mast.
He was riding the waves
As long as I could keep him in sight.

VIOLA *(giving him money)*: For saying that,
Here's gold. My own escape gives me hope
That he escaped, too.
Do you know this country?

CAPTAIN: Yes. I was born and raised here.

VIOLA: Who governs here?

CAPTAIN: A noble duke named Orsino.

VIOLA: Orsino! My father spoke of him.
He was a bachelor then.

CAPTAIN: And he still is—or was till recently.
A month ago, when I left, I heard rumors
That he sought the love of fair Olivia.

VIOLA: Who's she?

CAPTAIN: A virtuous maiden, the daughter of
A count who died a year ago. He left her in
The protection of his son, her brother,
Who died soon after that. For his dear love,
They say, she has given up the company
And even sight of men!

VIOLA: I wish I served that lady and could
Stay out of the public eye until I found out
Better what my situation is!

CAPTAIN: That will not be easy. She will not
Consider any pleas—not even the duke's.

VIOLA: You seem like a good man, Captain.
Will you—I'll pay you well—help me
Disguise who I am? I want to serve this duke.

You can present me as a young man to him.
It will be worth your trouble. I can sing, and
I can speak to him in many musical ways.
This will make me an attractive employee.
Whatever happens, time will tell.
Just be silent, will you? Well?

CAPTAIN: If silent I am unable to be,

Then may my eyes no longer see!

VIOLA: Thank you. *(She gestures.)* After you . . .
(They exit.)

Scene ❸

A room in Olivia's house. **Sir Toby Belch** and **Maria** enter.

SIR TOBY: What the devil does my niece mean,
To take the death of her brother like this?
I'm sure worrying isn't good for her health.

MARIA: Really, Sir Toby, you must come home earlier
at night. Your niece does not like your late
hours. Your drinking will be the end of you.
I heard my lady talk of it yesterday. She also
talked about a foolish knight that you brought
here one night to be her wooer.

SIR TOBY: Who? Sir Andrew Aguecheek?
He's the equal of any man in Illyria.

MARIA: What do you mean?

SIR TOBY: Why, he is rich!

MARIA: Perhaps. But his money will last only a year.
He's a fool and a spendthrift.

SIR TOBY: Shame on you for saying so! He plays the
violin, and he speaks three or four languages.
He has all nature's finest gifts.

MARIA: He has indeed, like a natural born idiot! Besides being a fool, he likes to argue. Luckily, he also has the gift of cowardice. That slows down his zest in arguing. Without that, he would quickly have the gift of a grave—or so say those with brains!

SIR TOBY: They are scoundrels who say so! Who are they?

MARIA: The same who say he's drunk every night in your company.

SIR TOBY: With drinking to the health of my niece! What, my girl? Speak of the devil—here comes Sir Andrew Aguecheek.

(**Sir Andrew Aguecheek** enters.)

SIR ANDREW: Sir Toby Belch! Greetings!

SIR TOBY *(hugging him):* Sweet Sir Andrew!

SIR ANDREW *(to Maria):* Bless you, fair shrew. *(He thinks he's paid a compliment.)*

MARIA *(trying not to laugh):* And you too, sir.

SIR TOBY: Accost her, Sir Andrew. Accost her.

SIR ANDREW *(confused by a new word):* What does that mean?

13

SIR TOBY *(winking)*: My niece's chambermaid!

SIR ANDREW *(misunderstanding)*: Dear Miss Accost, I'd like to know you better.

MARIA: My name is Mary, sir.

SIR ANDREW: Dear Miss Mary Accost—

SIR TOBY *(interrupting)*: You've got it wrong, knight. "Accost" means to make advances, take her on, flirt with her, attack her.

SIR ANDREW: My word, I wouldn't tackle her in this company. Is *that* what the word means?

MARIA *(turning to go)*: Goodbye, gentlemen.

(**Maria** exits.)

SIR TOBY: Oh, knight! You need a glass of wine. When have I ever seen you so put down? Why, my dear knight?

SIR ANDREW: Sir Toby, your niece will not see me. Even if she did, it's four to one she'd have nothing to do with me. The count himself, who lives near here, is wooing her.

SIR TOBY: She'll have nothing to do with the count. She won't marry above herself—either in

fortune, age, or intelligence.
I have heard her swear it. Nonsense!
You stand a good chance with her, man!

SIR ANDREW: I'll stay a month longer. After
all, I'm a fellow with a playful mind.
I love costume parties and dances, sometimes
both together.

SIR TOBY: Are you good at dancing, knight?

SIR ANDREW: As good as any man in Illyria,
provided he's my inferior. But I can't compare
with an experienced man.

SIR TOBY: How good are you at a reel, knight?

SIR ANDREW: Well, I think I can dance as neatly as
any man! *(He demonstrates, poorly.)*

SIR TOBY *(pretending to admire him)*: Why have
you been hiding all your talent? Why have
these gifts been kept behind a curtain? They
are likely to get dusty, like a painting. Why
don't you dance the reel on your way to church
and come home doing a fling? If I were you,
my very walk would be a jig. What are you
thinking? Is this the kind of world to hide

virtues in? Looking at the excellent shape of your leg, I'd say it was formed under the influence of a dancing star.

SIR ANDREW *(boasting)*: Yes, it is strong—and it does look good in a flame-colored stocking. Shall we do some reveling?

SIR TOBY: Of course! Let me see you dance. *(Sir Andrew begins to dance.)* Higher!
(Sir Andrew does his best.) Ha, ha! Excellent!

(**They** exit.)

Scene ❹ 🎧

A room in the duke's palace. **Valentine** enters with
Viola, who is dressed as a young man and now
known as Cesario.

VALENTINE: If the duke continues to favor you,

> Cesario, you are likely to be promoted soon.
>
> He has known you only three days, and already
>
> you are no stranger.

VIOLA: Thank you. Here comes the duke now.

(The **duke, Curio,** and **attendants** enter.)

DUKE: Has anyone seen Cesario?

VIOLA: Ready to serve you, my lord.

DUKE *(to his attendants):* Stand aside a moment. *(to*

> *Viola)* Cesario, you know everything.
>
> I have opened my secret soul to you.
>
> Therefore, young man, go to her.
>
> Stand at her doors, and tell them that your foot
>
> Will take root until you're asked to come in.

VIOLA: Surely, my noble lord,

> If she is as lost in her sorrow as they say,
>
> She will never let me in.

DUKE: Do not take no for an answer!

VIOLA: Suppose I do speak with her, my lord. What
   then?

DUKE: Oh, tell her of the passion of my love.
   Surprise her with talk of my deep devotion.
   It will be good for you to speak to her.
   She will listen better to a youth
   Than to an older messenger.

VIOLA: I do not think so, my lord.

DUKE: Dear boy, believe it.
   You are perfect for this affair.
   Do well in this, and I will reward you with
   A share of my fortune.

VIOLA: I'll do my best to woo your lady.
   (Aside) A difficult job! Whomever I woo,
   What I really want is to marry *you!*

Scene **5**

A room in Olivia's house. **Maria** and **Feste** enter.

MARIA: Either tell me where you have been, or I will not open my mouth to make any excuses for you. My lady will fire you for being gone so long.

FESTE: Well, let her! At least it's summer, so I won't freeze.

MARIA: Here comes my lady now. You'd better be thinking of a good excuse.

(**Maria** exits.)

FESTE *(as if in prayer):* Oh, Wit, if you please, help me be witty. Jesters who think they're witty often prove to be fools. Since I know I'm not witty, I may pass for a wise man. What's the old saying? "Better a witty fool than a foolish wit."

(**Olivia** and **Malvolio** enter, followed by **attendants**.)

God bless you, lady!

OLIVIA *(with a weary gesture):* Take the fool away.

FESTE *(to the attendants):* Didn't you hear her, fellows? Take the lady away!

OLIVIA: Don't talk nonsense. You have a dry wit. I've had enough of you. Besides, you're becoming dishonest.

FESTE: Two faults, madam, that drink and good advice will cure. Give the dry fool drink, and soon the fool is not dry. Tell the dishonest man to mend himself, and if he does, he is no longer dishonest. If he cannot mend himself, let a cheap tailor mend him. Anything that is mended is patched. Virtue that goes wrong is patched with sin. Sin that mends its ways is patched with virtue. If this simple logic works for you, fine. If not, what can be done about it? *(to attendants)* The lady said to take away the fool. Therefore, I say again, take her away.

OLIVIA: Sir, I told them to take *you* away.

FESTE: An error in the highest degree! Lady, "the hood doesn't make the monk." In other words, don't be deceived by my jester's clothing. Good lady, allow me to prove that you are a fool.

OLIVIA: Can you do it?

FESTE: Easily, good lady.

OLIVIA: Make your proof.

FESTE: I must ask you questions to do it, madam.

OLIVIA: Well, sir, for lack of anything better to do, I'll go along with you.

FESTE: My lady, why are you in mourning?

OLIVIA: Good fool, for my brother's death.

FESTE: I think his soul is in hell, my lady.

OLIVIA: I know his soul is in heaven, fool.

FESTE: The more fool you are, my lady, to mourn for your brother's soul being in heaven. *(to attendants)* Take away the fool, gentlemen.

OLIVIA *(to Malvolio)*: What do you think of this fool, Malvolio? Isn't he improving?

MALVOLIO: Yes, and he'll continue to do so, till he's in his death throes. Old age, which decays the wise, always makes fools even more foolish.

FESTE: May God send you, sir, a speedy old age, to increase your folly even more! Sir Toby will swear that I am no great wit, but he wouldn't take two cents to swear that you are not a fool.

OLIVIA: What do you say to that, Malvolio?

MALVOLIO: I am amazed that your ladyship takes delight in such an empty-headed rascal.

OLIVIA: Oh, you take yourself too seriously, and your judgment is poor. A kind person overlooks the faults in others.

(**Maria** returns.)

MARIA: Madam, there is at the gate a young gentleman who wishes to speak with you.

OLIVIA: From the Count Orsino, is he?

MARIA: I don't know, madam. He's a fair young man, with several attendants.

OLIVIA: Who of my people is keeping him waiting?

MARIA: Sir Toby, madam, your relative.

OLIVIA: Fetch Sir Toby away, please. He talks like a madman. Shame on him!

(**Maria** exits.)

You go, Malvolio. If he has a message from the count, tell him I am sick, or not at home, or say whatever you wish to get rid of him.

(**Malvolio** exits. **Olivia** turns to **Feste**.)

Now you see, sir, how people dislike your fooling.

22

FESTE: You have spoken for us jesters, madam, as if your eldest son were a fool. May God cram his skull with brains—because here comes one of your relatives who is not too bright.

(**Sir Toby Belch** enters.)

OLIVIA: Upon my honor, he's half drunk!
(to Sir Toby) What kind of person is at the gate, cousin?

SIR TOBY: A gentleman.

OLIVIA: A gentleman? What gentleman?

SIR TOBY: There's a gentleman here.
(He belches loudly.) Blame these pickled herrings!
(to Feste) Greetings, fool!

FESTE: Dear Sir Toby!

OLIVIA: Cousin, cousin, how do you come to have this dullness, this lethargy, so early?

SIR TOBY *(misunderstanding)*: Lechery! I defy lechery. There's someone at the gate.

OLIVIA: Yes, indeed. What sort of man is he?

SIR TOBY: Let him be the devil if he wishes, I don't care. It's all the same to me.

23

(**Sir Toby** exits.)

OLIVIA: What's a drunken man like, fool?

FESTE: Like a drowning man, a fool, and a madman.
One drink too many makes him foolish, the
second makes him mad, and the third drowns
him.

OLIVIA: Go and find the coroner. Let him
take my cousin, for he's in the third degree of
drink. He's drowned.
Go and look after him.

FESTE: He's only at the mad stage, madam. The fool
will look after the madman.

(**Feste** exits. **Malvolio** returns.)

MALVOLIO: Madam, the young fellow at the door
swears he will speak with you. I told him you
were sick. He said he already knew that, and
for that reason has come to speak with you. I
told him you were asleep. He claims to already
know that, too, and for that reason comes to
speak to you. What can I say to him, lady? He
has an answer for everything.

OLIVIA: Tell him that he shall not speak with me.

MALVOLIO: He has been told so. He says he'll stand at your door like a flagpole, or prop up a bench— but he will speak to you.

OLIVIA: What kind of man is he?

MALVOLIO: Why, of the human race . . .

OLIVIA: What type of man?

MALVOLIO: Very rude. He'll speak to you, whether you wish it or not.

OLIVIA: What's he like, and how old is he?

MALVOLIO: Not old enough to be a man,
nor young enough to be a boy.
He is very good-looking.

OLIVIA: Let him come in. Call my gentlewoman.

MALVOLIO: Gentlewoman! My lady calls.

(**Malvolio** exits. **Maria** returns.)

OLIVIA: Give me my veil. Throw it over my face.
We'll hear Orsino's message once again.

(**Viola**, dressed as **Cesario**, enters.)

VIOLA: The lady of the house, which is she?

OLIVIA: I'll answer for her. What is it?

VIOLA *(beginning her prepared speech)*: Most radiant, exquisite, and unmatched beauty . . . *(breaking off)* Please, tell me if this is the lady of the house, for I never saw her. I'd hate to waste my speech. Apart from the fact that it is very well-written, I have worked hard to learn it by heart. *(Maria cannot keep from laughing.)* Please, do not laugh at me. I am very sensitive.

OLIVIA: Where have you come from, sir?

VIOLA: I can say little more than what I've learned, and that question isn't in my script. Gentle madam, give me some small assurance that you are the lady of the house.

OLIVIA: Are you an actor?

VIOLA: No. And yet, I swear that I am not what I appear to be. Are you the lady of the house?

OLIVIA: I am.

VIOLA: Then I will go on with my speech in your praise. After that, I will get to the heart of my message.

OLIVIA: Get to the point. Forget the praise.

VIOLA: I worked hard to learn it, and it's poetic.

OLIVIA: It's all the more likely to be fake. I beg you to keep it to yourself. I heard you were brazen at my gates. I allowed you to come in, more to wonder at you than to hear you. If you're mad, be gone. If you're sane, be brief. I'm not in the mood to have such a silly conversation. Say what's on your mind.

VIOLA: I am a messenger.

OLIVIA: Surely, you must have some hideous message to deliver, when the formalities are so complicated. What is it?

VIOLA: It is for your ears alone. I bring you no declaration of war, no demands for taxes. I hold an olive branch in my hand. My words are full of peace, not argument.

OLIVIA: Yet you began rudely. What are you? What do you want?

VIOLA: I was rude because I was treated rudely. What I am and what I want are as secret as virginity. To your ears, divine; To any other's, profane.

OLIVIA *(to Maria)*: Leave us alone. I'll hear this "divinity."

ACT 1
SCENE 5

27

(**Maria** exits.)

VIOLA: Most sweet lady . . .

OLIVIA: Where does your text come from?

VIOLA: Orsino's heart.

OLIVIA: His heart? In what chapter of his heart?

VIOLA: To answer in the same style: Chapter One of his heart.

OLIVIA: Oh, I have already read it. It is heresy. Have you anything else to say?

VIOLA: Good madam, let me see your face.

OLIVIA: Has your master told you to negotiate with my face? Well, we will draw the curtain and show you the picture. *(She lifts her veil.)* Isn't it a good likeness?

VIOLA: Excellently done, if it's all God's work.

OLIVIA: It is protected, sir. It will endure wind and weather.

VIOLA: It is beauty well-blended. The colors
Were done by Nature's own sweet hand.
Lady, you are the cruelest woman alive,
If you will take these gifts to the grave,
And leave the world no copy.

OLIVIA: Oh, sir, I will not be so hard-hearted.

I'll publish various lists of my beauty.

It will be inventoried, and every detail

Labeled as I wish. Item: two lips, fairly red.

Item: two gray eyes with lids to them.

Item: one neck, one chin, and so forth.

Were you sent here to praise me?

VIOLA: I see what you are!

You are too proud. But, even if you are

The devil, you are beautiful!

My lord and master loves you.

OLIVIA: How does he love me?

VIOLA: With great adoration and many tears.

With groans that thunder out their love.

With sighs of fire.

OLIVIA: Your lord knows my feelings.

I cannot love him. But I believe he is virtuous. I
     know he is noble, wealthy, and youthful.

He is well-regarded, free-spirited, educated, and
     brave. He is also said to be gracious.

Yet I cannot love him.

He should have accepted my answer long ago.

VIOLA: If I loved you as my master does,
   With such suffering and agony,
   I would find no sense in your answer.
   I would not understand it.

OLIVIA: Why, what would you do?

VIOLA: I'd make myself a cabin at your gate,
   And call upon my loved one in the house.
   I'd write devoted songs of hopeless love,
   And sing them loud, even in the dead of night.
   I'd shout your name to the echoing hills,
   And make the echoes on the air
   Cry out "Olivia!" Oh, you couldn't live
   On this earth without feeling pity for me.

OLIVIA: In your case, you might succeed.
   What is your background?

VIOLA: Better than my present situation.
   I am a gentleman.

OLIVIA: Go back to your lord. I cannot love him. Tell
   him to send no more messages—
   Unless, by chance, you come to me again
   To tell me how he takes it. Goodbye.

I thank you for the trouble you have taken.
(She hands Viola some money.) Spend this for
  me.

VIOLA *(refusing)*: I am no paid messenger, lady.
  Keep your money. It is my master,
  Not myself, who lacks reward.
  May the man you love have a heart of stone,
  And let your passion, like my master's,
  Be treated with contempt!
  Farewell, you cruel beauty!

(**Viola** exits.)

OLIVIA: What is your background?
  "Better than my present situation.
    I am a gentleman."
  I'll swear an oath you are!
  Your voice, face, limbs, action, and spirit
  Indicate a five-star pedigree. *(She thinks.)*
  Not too fast . . . softly, softly! Now if the master
    were the man . . . what then?
  Can one fall in love so fast?
  I think I feel this youth's perfections
  Creeping their way in through my eyes.

Well, let it be. *(She calls out.)* Hello there!
Malvolio! *(She takes a ring off her finger.)*

(**Malvolio** returns.)

MALVOLIO: Here, madam, at your service.

OLIVIA *(handing him the ring)*: Run after that
Rude messenger fellow, the count's man.
He left this ring behind him,
Whether I wanted it or not.
Tell him I won't have it!
Tell him not to mince words with his lord
Nor give him false hopes. I am not for him.
If the youth will come this way tomorrow,
I'll give him my reasons. Hurry, Malvolio!

MALVOLIO: Madam, I will.

(**Malvolio** exits.)

OLIVIA: I don't know what I'm doing!
I'm afraid my eyes may be fooling me.
Fate, show your power.
We do not control our own destiny.
What must be, must be!

(**Olivia** exits.)

32

ACT 2

Summary

安東尼奧從船難中拯救西巴斯辛後,他冒著危險隨著他的新朋友去晉見奧西諾。同時,當馬伏里奧試圖將戒指還給薇奧拉時,薇奧拉拒絕收下戒指。薇奧拉懷疑奧麗維婭對西薩里奧有好感,卻對這一切束手無策。

在馬伏里奧斥責托比和安德魯飲酒作樂後,愚蠢的安德魯建議與馬伏里奧一決死戰,但瑪利婭有更好的點子:她建議對馬伏里奧惡作劇——偽造奧麗維婭的筆跡寫一封情書給馬伏里奧。托比和安德魯立刻欣然答應,他們躲在樹叢後面偷看馬伏里奧讀信並幻想與奧麗維婭交往的癡情傻樣。

Scene ❶ 🎧

The seacoast. **Antonio** and **Sebastian** enter.

ANTONIO: Can't I go with you?

SEBASTIAN: Forgive me, no. I've had bad luck lately.
My bad luck might affect yours.
Let me bear my troubles alone.

ANTONIO: Tell me where you are going.

SEBASTIAN: No, really, sir. My planned trip is
nothing but wandering. I see that you are too
polite to insist on information that I wish to
keep to myself. But good manners require
me to tell you that Sebastian is my real name,
though I said it was Roderigo. My father was
Sebastian of Messaline, who died and left me
and my twin sister behind. We were born
within the same hour. If the heavens had
wished it, we would have died the same way!
But you, sir, changed that. About an hour or so
before you rescued me from the sea, my sister
drowned.

ANTONIO: How terrible!

SEBASTIAN: Even though she looked like me, many people thought she was beautiful.
I will say this about her: She had a beautiful mind. Now she is drowned, sir, in saltwater. *(He chokes back a tear.)* I seem to drown her memory in salty tears.

ANTONIO *(realizing Sebastian is a gentleman):* Pardon me, sir, for my humble hospitality.

SEBASTIAN: Oh, good Antonio, forgive me for being so much trouble.

ANTONIO: If you don't want me to die for my love, let me be your servant.

SEBASTIAN: Unless you want to undo what you have done—that is, kill the man you have just rescued—don't ask that. For now, goodbye. My heart has such tender feelings for you, the least thing might make me cry. I am going to the court of Count Orsino. Farewell.

(Sebastian exits.)

ANTONIO: May the gods go with you!

　　I have many enemies in Orsino's court,

　　Or else I would follow you there.
　　(He turns to go, and then stops to think again.)

　　But come what may, I am so fond of you

　　That danger seems like fun—so I will go!

(**Antonio** exits.)

Scene ❷ 🎧

The street. **Viola** and **Malvolio** enter.

MALVOLIO: Weren't you with the Countess Olivia just now? *(offering a ring)* She returns this ring to you, sir. You might have saved me trouble by taking it away yourself. Please assure your lord that she wants nothing to do with him. And one more thing: You must never be so bold as to come again on his affairs—unless it is to report how he takes this. *(throwing the ring on the ground)* Take it back.

VIOLA *(stopping to think, and then realizing the situation)***:** I don't want the ring back.

MALVOLIO: Sir, you rudely threw it to her, and she wants me to return it the same way. If it is worth stooping for, there it is where you can see it. If not, let it belong to whoever finds it.

(**Malvolio** exits.)

VIOLA: I gave her no ring. What does she mean? Heaven forbid that my looks charmed her! She looked me over so closely that

I thought her eyes had tied her tongue.

She loves me, that's sure. Her passion

Invites me through this rude messenger.

(scornfully) She won't have my lord's ring!

Why, he didn't send her one!

If it's true that I'm the man she loves,

Poor lady, she'd be better off loving a dream.

My disguise is a form of wickedness

That helps the devil do his work.

How easy it is for attractive but false men

To work their way into women's hearts!

Alas, our weakness is the cause, not we.

What we are made of, that we must be.

(She thinks.) How will this turn out?

My master loves her dearly,

And I, poor devil, am just as fond of him.

Not knowing, she seems to dote on him.

What will become of this? As a man,

I have no chance of my master's love.

Oh time, you must untangle this, not I.

It is too hard a knot for me to untie!

(**Viola** exits.)

Scene ❸ 🎧

A room in Olivia's house. **Sir Toby Belch** and **Sir Andrew Aguecheek** enter. They are both drunk.

SIR TOBY: Come on, Sir Andrew. Not to be in bed after midnight is to be up early. You know that.

SIR ANDREW: No, upon my word, I do not know that. To be up late is to be up late.

SIR TOBY: That's false logic. I hate it as I hate an unfilled glass! To be up after midnight, and to go to bed then is early. Aren't our lives made up of the four elements of fire, water, air, and earth?

SIR ANDREW: So they say. But I think it really consists of eating and drinking.

SIR TOBY: You are a scholar! Let us therefore eat and drink. *(Calling)* Maria, I say! Some wine!

(**Feste** enters.)

FESTE: How goes it, my friends?

SIR TOBY: Welcome, fool. Now let's have a song.

SIR ANDREW: Upon my word, the fool has an excellent voice. *(to Feste)* You were in

rare form last night! The entertainment was
very good. Here's some money.
Let's have a song.

FESTE: Would you like a love song, or a song about
how good life is?

SIR TOBY: A love song, a love song.

FESTE *(singing as he plays his lute)*: Oh, mistress
mine, where are you roaming?
Oh, stay and hear. Your true love's coming,

Who can sing both high and low.
Go no further, pretty sweeting;
Journeys end in lovers meeting,
Every wise man's son does know.

SIR ANDREW: Extremely good, indeed!

SIR TOBY: Good, good.

FESTE *(singing)*: What is love? It's not hereafter.
Present mirth has present laughter.
What's to come is still unsure.
In delay there lies no plenty.
Then come kiss me, sweet and twenty.
Youth's a stuff will not endure!

SIR ANDREW: A sweet voice, as I am a true knight.

SIR TOBY: Shall we sing a song together?

SIR ANDREW: If you love me, let's do it. Let's sing "You knave." You start, fool. It begins, "Hold your peace."

FESTE: I shall never begin if I hold my peace.

SIR ANDREW: That's good! Come on, let's begin.

(They sing. **Maria** enters.)

MARIA: What a racket you're making! If my lady
hasn't told her steward Malvolio to throw you
out, don't ever trust me again.

SIR TOBY: My lady's a prude. Malvolio
Is an old woman, and—
(singing) Three merry men we be!
Tilly-valley, lady.

FESTE: I swear, the knight's in rare form.

SIR ANDREW: Yes, he does well enough if he's in the
mood. And so do I. He does it with better style,
but I do it more naturally.

SIR TOBY *(singing)*: Oh, the twelfth day of
December—

MARIA: For the love of God, *quiet!*

(**Malvolio** enters.)

MALVOLIO: Gentlemen, are you mad, or what? Have
you no sense or good manners?
To raise such a squawking ruckus
Makes an alehouse of my lady's home. Have
you no respect?
Sir Toby, I must be straight with you.
My lady welcomes you as her kinsman,

But she doesn't like your bad behavior.
Stay if you can behave yourself. If not—
And if it would please you to leave—she
Is very willing to see you go.

SIR TOBY: Are you any more than a steward? Just
because *you* are virtuous,
Must we be, too?

FESTE: Yes, by Saint Anne! The fun is over!

SIR TOBY: Is it really? Go, sir, polish the
leash my lady keeps around your neck. *(calling)*
More wine, Maria!

MALVOLIO: Miss Mary, if you valued my lady's good
opinion, you would not supply the drink for
this rude behavior. *(shaking his fist)* She shall
know of it, by this hand.

(**Malvolio** exits.)

MARIA: Go shake your ears, you donkey!

SIR ANDREW: That's as good as making a fool of a
man by not showing up for a duel!

SIR TOBY: Challenge Malvolio, sir knight!
I'll deliver it to him in person!

MARIA: Sweet Sir Toby, be patient for tonight. Since the count's young man visited my Lady today, she's been very touchy.
Leave Malvolio to me! I can make him
Into a byword for stupidity.

SIR TOBY: Tell us how! Tell us how!

MARIA: He thinks he's so full of excellence that
Everyone who sees him must love him.
That weakness will be his downfall.

SIR TOBY: What will you do?

MARIA: I will drop some love letters in his path. The letters will lovingly describe the color of his beard, the shape of his leg, the way he walks, and the expression in his eyes. I can write just like my lady. Sometimes we cannot even remember who wrote what.

SIR TOBY: Excellent! I smell a rat.

SIR ANDREW: I smell it, too.

SIR TOBY: He will think the letters come from
My niece, who must be in love with him.

MARIA: I am betting on a horse of that color.
I am sure of it.

SIR ANDREW: Oh, yes, it will be admirable!

MARIA: Royal sport, I guarantee you.
I know my medicine will work with
him. You two, along with Fabian, can hide
where he will find the letter.
Then watch him interpret it. But for tonight: to
bed, and farewell.

(**Maria** exits.)

SIR ANDREW: Believe me, she's a good one!

SIR TOBY: And she adores me. What do you think of
that?

SIR ANDREW: I was adored once, too.

SIR TOBY: I'll go heat some sherry. It's too late to go
to bed now. Come on, knight!

(**Sir Toby** and **Sir Andrew** exit.)

Scene 4 🎧

A room in the duke's palace. The **duke, Viola, Curio,** and **others** enter.

DUKE: Good morning! Let's have music.
(to Viola) Please, good Cesario, sing
That quaint, old song we heard last night.
Come, just one verse.

CURIO: If it pleases your lordship, the one
who should sing it is Feste, the jester. He's
around the house somewhere.

DUKE: Seek him out, and play the tune
meanwhile. *(Curio exits. Music plays.)*
(to Viola) Come here, boy.
If you ever fall in love,
In the sweet pangs of it, remember me:
For all true lovers act just as I do—
Unstable and fickle in everything but
Their obsession with the creature who is loved.
How do you like this tune?

VIOLA: It gives an exact echo of the throne
Where love sits.

DUKE: You speak like an expert!
I'd bet that, even though you are young,

You have your eye on someone you love.
Isn't that so, boy?

VIOLA: A little—if I may say so.

DUKE: What kind of woman is she?

VIOLA: She looks like you.

DUKE: She is not worth you, then.
How old is she?

VIOLA: About as old as you, my lord.

DUKE: Too old, by heaven! The woman
Should always marry someone older,
So she can adjust herself to suit him.
Then she will always keep a steady place
In her husband's heart.
For, boy, no matter how we flatter ourselves,
Men's affections are unstable,
Full of desire and fickle—
Sooner lost and won, than women's are!

VIOLA: I think you are right, my lord.

DUKE: Then let your love be younger than you,
Or your affection will not last.
For women are like roses, fair flowers
Once displayed, that fade that very hour.

VIOLA: And so they are. Alas, that it is so,
To die, just as they to perfection grow!

(**Curio** and **Feste** enter again.)

DUKE: Oh, fellow, come on—
The song you sang last night.

FESTE: Are you ready, sir?

DUKE: Yes. Please sing.

FESTE *(singing along to the music)*: Come away,
come away, death.
And in sad cypress let me be laid.
Fly away, fly away, breath.
I am slain by a fair cruel maid.
My shroud of white, stuck all with yew,
Oh, prepare it!

DUKE *(giving him money)*: For your pains.

FESTE: No pains, sir. I take pleasure in singing.

DUKE: I'll pay for your pleasure, then.

FESTE: True, sir. Pleasure must be paid for at one
time or another.

DUKE: That's enough of that!

FESTE: May the gods protect you. Farewell.

(**Feste** exits.)

DUKE: The rest of you may leave.

(**Curio** and **attendants** exit.)

DUKE: *(to Viola)* Once more, Cesario,
Go to that same cruel lady.
Tell her my noble love puts no value on large
    estates of dirty land. Tell her that
What attracts my soul to her is her beauty,
In which she's a miracle and a queen of gems.

VIOLA: But what if she cannot love you, sir?

DUKE: I do not accept that answer.

VIOLA: Truly, but you must. Suppose that some
    lady—as perhaps there is—
Loves you as much as you love Olivia.
You cannot love her, and tell her so.
Mustn't she then accept your answer?

DUKE: No woman's heart can bear so strong
A passion as love gives my heart.
No woman's heart is big enough for it!
Women lack staying power.
Alas, their love may be called appetite.
It's not driven by emotion but by taste.
But my appetite is as hungry as the sea

And can digest as much. Do not compare
The love a woman can have for me
With the love I have for Olivia.

VIOLA: Yes, but I know— *(She breaks off, afraid to reveal herself.)*

DUKE: What do you know?

VIOLA: How well women may love men.
In fact, they are as true of heart as we.
My father had a daughter who loved a man—
As I might—if I were a woman—
Love your lordship.

DUKE: And what's her story?

VIOLA: A blank, my lord.
She never revealed her love,
But let her secret, like a worm in the bud,
Feed on her rosy cheek. She pined in thought,
And sickened with grief. Wasn't this love?
We men say more and swear more, but indeed
Our behaviors are not sincere.
We tend to vow a lot, but love little.

DUKE: But did your sister die of her love, my boy?

VIOLA: I am all the daughters that my father has,
And all the brothers, too—
But I may be wrong about that.
(She's still hoping that Sebastian didn't drown.)
Sir, shall I go to this lady?

DUKE: Yes, that's the idea. *(giving Viola a jewel)*
Go to her quickly. Give her this jewel.
Say that my love cannot be denied.

(**Duke** and **Viola** exit.)

Scene ❺ 🎧⑫

Olivia's garden. **Sir Toby Belch, Sir Andrew Aguecheek,** and **Fabian** enter.

SIR TOBY: Come along, Mister Fabian.

FABIAN: I'm coming. If I miss a minute of this sport, may I be boiled to death in misery!

SIR TOBY: Won't you be glad to see the mean, rascally dog come to great shame?

FABIAN: I will rejoice, man!

(**Maria** enters.)

SIR TOBY: Here comes the little villain! How are things, my golden one?

MARIA: All three of you, hide behind the hedge.
Malvolio's coming! He's been in the sun,
Practicing bows to his own shadow.
For the love of mockery, watch him!
This letter will make an idiot of him.
Hide, in the name of practical joking!

(The men hide themselves as **Maria** throws down a letter. Then she exits and **Malvolio** enters.)

MALVOLIO: Everything is just a matter of luck. Maria once said that Olivia liked me.

I've heard hint that if she ever loved anyone, it would be someone like me. Besides, she treats me with more respect than any of the others. What should I think about that?

SIR TOBY: What a conceited rogue!

FABIAN: *Shhh!* Thinking makes him a rare peacock. Look how he struts under his raised feathers! Now he's deeply in thought.
Imagination is swelling his head.

MALVOLIO: I can see myself sitting in my chair of state—

SIR TOBY (*angrily*): Oh, if I only had a stone to hit him in the eye!

MALVOLIO: —calling my servants to me, in my fancy velvet gown, having come from a daybed, where I've left Olivia sleeping—

SIR TOBY (*more angrily*): Fire and brimstone!

FABIAN: Oh, quiet, quiet.

MALVOLIO: —I'd send for my kinsman Toby.

SIR TOBY *(even more angrily)*: Bolts and shackles!

FABIAN: Oh, quiet, quiet!

MALVOLIO: Seven of my people obediently go to get him. I frown meanwhile, maybe wind up my watch or play with some rich jewel. Toby comes and bows to me.

SIR TOBY *(totally outraged by now)*: Shall this fellow be allowed to live?

FABIAN: Even if wild horses tried to drag words out of us, be silent now!

MALVOLIO: I extend my hand to him like this *(he stretches forth a limp hand)*, holding back my familiar smile with a look of authority—

SIR TOBY: And doesn't Toby hit you in the mouth then?

MALVOLIO: —saying, "Cousin Toby, since good fortune has given me your niece, I have the right to say this."

SIR TOBY: What? What?

MALVOLIO: "You must stop your drunkenness."

SIR TOBY: Away, you scab!

FABIAN: Be patient, or we'll give our game away.

MALVOLIO: "Besides, you waste your precious time with a foolish knight."

SIR ANDREW: He's talking about me, I tell you!

MALVOLIO: "One Sir Andrew."

SIR ANDREW: I *knew* it was me. Many people call me a fool.

MALVOLIO *(picking up the letter)*: What's this?

FABIAN: Now the bird is near the trap.

SIR TOBY: May he be inspired to read it aloud!

MALVOLIO: By my life, this is my lady's handwriting. *(Reading) To the unknown beloved: this letter and my good wishes.* Her very phrases. *(He breaks the wax seal.)*
It has her personal seal on it. Yes, it's from my lady, all right. To whom has it been sent?

FABIAN: This will convince him, heart and soul.

MALVOLIO *(reading)*: *God knows I love,*
But who?
Lips, do not move,
No man must know.
What if it should be you, Malvolio?

SIR TOBY: Be hanged, you braggart!

MALVOLIO: *Silence cuts me like a knife,*
M, O, A, I, does rule my life.

SIR TOBY: Excellent woman, I say.

FABIAN: What poison she has served him!

SIR TOBY: And how quickly he takes the bait!

MALVOLIO: Now she writes in prose.
I may command where I adore.
Why, she may command me! I serve her—she is

my lady. What do those letters mean? M, O, A, I—all those letters are in my name, but not in that order.

If this letter falls into your hand, consider. By the chance of fortune, I am above you, but do not be afraid of greatness! Some are born great, some achieve greatness, and some have greatness thrust upon them. The fates offer their helping hands. Let your courage and spirit embrace them. To prepare yourself for what you are likely to be, cast off your humble exterior and appear fresh. Be openly hostile to a certain kinsman and rude with servants. Let your speech be about lofty matters. Be original. She who sighs for you gives you this advice. Remember who complimented you on your yellow stockings. I say, remember. Go on, your fortune is made, if you want it to be. If not, you can stay a steward forever, the friend of servants, and not worthy to touch Fortune's fingers. Farewell. She who would be your servant.

–The Fortunate-Unhappy

This is as plain as daylight! I will be proud.
I will read important authors, I will clash with
Sir Toby. I will avoid my common friends.
Everything points to this: My lady loves me.
She did praise my yellow stockings recently. In
this way *(he waves the letter)*, she tells me of
her love and encourages me to act in ways she
likes. I thank my lucky stars that I am so lucky
in love. I will be aloof and proud, in yellow
stockings as fast as I can put them on.
(He turns the letter over.) Here is a postscript:
*You cannot help but know who I am. If you love
me, too, show it by smiling. You have such a
lovely smile. So in my presence, smile, my dear
sweetheart, I beg you.*
I will smile. I will do all she asks.
(**Malvolio** exits.)

FABIAN: I wouldn't give up my part in this sport for a pension paid by the shah of Persia!

SIR TOBY: I could marry the girl for this hoax.

SIR ANDREW: So could I!

SIR TOBY: And ask no other dowry from her but another such joke.

(**Maria** enters.)

FABIAN: Here comes our noble jokester!

SIR TOBY: When he comes out of his dream,
He'll go mad, for sure!

MARIA: Tell the truth. Do you think it worked?

SIR TOBY: Without question!

MARIA: If you want to see the joke play out, watch him when he first sees my lady.

He will come to her in yellow stockings, a color she hates. He will smile at her, which will be so opposite to her mood. You know how inclined she is to sadness. How annoyed she will be! If you want to see it, follow me!

SIR TOBY: Lead on, you excellent jokester!

SIR ANDREW: I'll go, too.

(**All** exit.)

ACT 3

Summary

西薩里奧再次替奧西諾公爵向奧麗維婭示愛，而這次，奧麗維婭坦言她對西薩里奧的愛意，她給他一枚珠寶當作愛的信物。西薩里奧離去，鬱鬱寡歡並感到十分困惑。同時，安德魯爵士在追求的過程中受挫，托比爵士認為奧麗維婭只是想讓他感到忌妒，建議他對西薩里奧立下一決死戰的戰書以證明他對奧麗維婭的一片真心。

同時，馬伏里奧因照著瑪利婭信中的蠢建議而行事，舉手投足都讓奧麗維婭感到噁心——他穿著黃色的長襪，並突然微笑。托比爵士、費比恩和瑪利婭假裝他被邪靈附身，並將他關在黑暗的屋內。

托比爵士鼓吹安德魯爵士進行比劍，也告訴他和西薩里奧對手是多麼強悍。接著，安東尼奧以為西薩里奧是西巴斯辛，打斷這場爭鬥，告訴安德魯爵士他願意替朋友上場。但此時，身為伊利里亞通緝犯的安東尼奧卻被執法人員所逮捕。由於安東尼奧之前將錢袋借給西巴斯辛，當他聽見西薩里奧宣稱對這筆錢一無所知時感到心碎，因為他需要這筆錢來繳交保釋金。聽見安東尼奧提到「西巴斯辛」這個名字，西薩里奧（薇奧拉）迅速起身去找他。

Scene ❶ 🎧

Olivia's garden. **Viola** enters, and **Feste** with a small drum.

VIOLA: Greetings, friend, and your music. Do you live by your drumming?

FESTE: No, sir, I live by the church.

VIOLA: Are you a preacher?

FESTE: No, sir. I live by the church, for I live in my house, and my house is near the church.

VIOLA: So you could just as well say the king lives by begging, if a beggar lives near him. Or the church is near your drum if the drum happens to be near the church.

FESTE: You said it, sir! Such are the times! A sentence is just a kid glove to a man with a quick wit. It can so easily be turned inside out!

VIOLA: I can see you're a merry fellow and care about nothing.

FESTE: Not so, sir. I do care for something. But upon my conscience, sir, I do not care for you. If that's caring about nothing, sir, I wish it would make you invisible.

VIOLA: Aren't you the Lady Olivia's fool?

FESTE: No, indeed, sir. Lady Olivia does not enjoy entertainment. She will not keep a fool, sir, until she is married. A fool is to a husband as a sardine is to a herring— the husband's the bigger. I am, indeed, not her fool, but her corrupter of words.

VIOLA: I saw you recently at Count Orsino's.

FESTE: I think I saw your wise self there, too.

VIOLA: If you make fun of me, I'll stay with you no longer. Wait. *(She looks in her purse.)* Here's something for you. *(She gives him some money.)*
Is your lady inside?

FESTE: The lady is inside, sir. I will let her know you are here.

(Feste exits.)

VIOLA: He's wise enough to be a paid fool.
And, to do that well, requires intelligence.
He must observe the moods of those
He jokes about. This is a job requiring as much
   hard work

As the profession of a wise man.

When it's done intelligently, his fooling

Is fit and proper. But when a wise man

Stoops to folly, he ruins his reputation.

(**Sir Toby Belch** and **Sir Andrew Aguecheek** enter.)

SIR TOBY: God be with you, gentleman.

VIOLA: And you, sir.

SIR TOBY: Will you come into the house? My niece
   wishes for you to enter, if your trade is with her.

VIOLA: I do wish to see your niece, sir.

(**Olivia** and **Maria** come out of the house to meet her.
Viola begins one of her prepared speeches.)

Most excellent accomplished lady,

May the heavens rain favors on you!

I've a message meant for your ears alone.

OLIVIA *(to the others)*: Let the garden door be shut,
   and then leave us alone.

(**Sir Toby, Sir Andrew,** and **Maria** exit.)

Give me your hand, sir. *(She offers hers.)*

VIOLA: *(taking it and bowing)*: Fair princess,
   I am your humble servant, Cesario.

OLIVIA: My servant, sir!

You are servant to the Count Orsino.

VIOLA: As he is yours. And what is his
  Must also belong to you. Your servant's
  Servant is your servant, madam.

OLIVIA: As for him, I don't think about him.
  As for his thoughts, I wish they were blanks
  Rather than filled with me!

VIOLA: Madam, I am here to make you think
  More kindly of him.

OLIVIA: Oh, please, I beg you,
  Don't ever speak of him again.
  But if you insist on pleading,
  I'd rather hear it
  Than music from the heavens.
  After your last enchanting visit,
  I sent a ring after you. In doing that,
  I wronged myself, my servant, and,
  I fear—you. I must accept your bad opinion
  Of me for forcing that ring on you in
  Such a shameful way. What must you think?

VIOLA: I pity you.

OLIVIA: That's a step toward love.

VIOLA: No, not even a small step. It's well-known
That very often we pity enemies.

OLIVIA: Well, then, I think it's time I learn
To smile again.

(A clock strikes.)

The clock reminds me of the waste of time.
Fear not, good youth. I will not pursue you.
And yet, when you come to maturity,
Your wife will have a good man.
(She points toward the setting sun.) There is
your route: duc west.

VIOLA: Then westward ho!
Blessings and a good life to your ladyship.
You have no message for my lord?

OLIVIA: Stay a moment. May I ask you
What you think of me?

VIOLA: *(speaking in a riddle):* That you think you
are what you are not. *(She means, "You think
you love a man, but you do not.")*

OLIVIA *(assuming Viola is being rude):* If I think so,
I think the same of you. *(She means,
"I think you are rude.")*

VIOLA: Then you think right. I am not what I appear
to be. *(She means, "I'm a woman.")*

OLIVIA: I wish you were as I want you to be! *(She
means, "I wish you were my husband!")*

VIOLA: Would it be better than I am now?
I hope so, for you are making me look silly.

OLIVIA: *(to herself):* Oh, how handsome he looks
When he is angry! Love that tries to hide itself
Is exposed sooner than the crime of murder.
Love is as plain as daylight.
(aloud) Cesario, by the roses of the spring,
Maidenhood, honor, truth, and everything,
I love you so much that I cannot hide it.
Don't draw any wrong conclusions from my
Words of love. You have given me
No reason to woo you. Think of it this way:
Love that's sought after is good, but
Love that is given unsought is better.

VIOLA: I swear that my heart, my loyalty,
And my truth belong to me. No woman has,

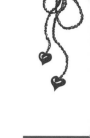

Or ever will have, a share in it, except me.
And so goodbye, good madam. I'll never again
Plead with you for my tearful master.

OLIVIA: Do come again. Maybe you'll be able
To move my heart to welcome his love.

(**Olivia** and **Viola** exit.)

Scene ❷ 〔14〕

A room in Olivia's house. **Sir Toby Belch, Sir Andrew Aguecheek,** and **Fabian** enter.

SIR ANDREW: No, I won't stay any longer.

SIR TOBY: But why, Sir Andrew?

SIR ANDREW: Well, I saw your niece being nicer to the count's servant than she has ever been to me. I saw it in the garden.

SIR TOBY: Did she see you there, old boy?

SIR ANDREW: As plain as I see you now.

FABIAN: Then it is clear that she did it just to make you jealous. You should have picked a fight with the youth. Now you look weak in her eyes. You'll have to do something soon.

SIR TOBY: Challenge the count's servant to a duel. Hurt him in eleven places. My niece will get to hear of it. A report of your courage will raise her opinion of you.

FABIAN: There is no other way, Sir Andrew.

SIR ANDREW: Will either of you deliver the challenge to him?

SIR TOBY: Go, write it in a strong handwriting. Be sharp and to the point. Off you go!

SIR ANDREW: Where shall I find you?

SIR TOBY: We'll meet you at the writing room. Go.

(**Sir Andrew** exits.)

FABIAN: He's your dear little puppet, Sir Toby.

SIR TOBY: I have been dear to him, lad—I've cost him some two thousand pounds or so.

FABIAN: We shall have quite a letter from him. Will you deliver it?

SIR TOBY: If I don't, never trust me again. And I'll do my best to get the youth to respond, though I think even oxen and ropes couldn't pull them together.

FABIAN: And his opponent, the youth, has no mark of cruelty in his face.

(**Maria** enters.)

SIR TOBY: Look, here comes our young bird.

MARIA: If you want a big laugh, follow me. That idiot Malvolio is wearing yellow stockings! He obeys every point in the letter that I wrote. He smiles until his face cracks. You've never seen such a sight! I can hardly resist hurling things at him. I know my lady will strike him. If she does, he'll smile and take it as a great favor.

SIR TOBY: Come on, take us to him!

(**All** exit.)

Scene **3** 🎧

A street. **Antonio** and **Sebastian** enter.

SEBASTIAN: I didn't mean to trouble you,
But since you enjoy putting yourself out,
I won't scold you anymore.

ANTONIO: I couldn't stay behind. I worried
About your safety. These lands
Often prove dangerous to a stranger
Without a guide or a friend.

SEBASTIAN: My kind Antonio!
I can make no other answer but thanks.
If I were as rich as I am indebted to you,
You would be richly rewarded.
What shall we do?
Shall we go see the sights of this town?

ANTONIO: Tomorrow, sir. It's best to find your
lodgings first.

SEBASTIAN: I am not tired, and it's still very early.
Let's do some sightseeing.

ANTONIO: If I may be excused—I walk
These streets in some danger.
Once, in a sea fight against the count's ships,
I played a big part. So big, in fact,

That if I were found here, I'd have no chance.

SEBASTIAN: You killed many of his people?

ANTONIO: The offense was not so bloody.
    It could be settled by repaying what we took
    From them. In fact, in the interest of trade,
    Most of our city's people did.
    I'm the only one who didn't.
    For that—if I'm found here—I shall
        pay dearly.

SEBASTIAN: Don't walk about too openly, then.

ANTONIO: Here's my purse. It's best to lodge
    In the south suburbs, at the Elephant Inn.
    I'll order our meal while you go sightseeing.
    You'll find me there.

SEBASTIAN: Why should I take your purse?

ANTONIO: Perhaps you'll see some souvenir
    You'd like to buy. I don't imagine you have
    Much extra money for luxuries, sir.

SEBASTIAN: I'll carry your purse and leave you for an
    hour.

ANTONIO: To the Elephant . . .

SEBASTIAN: I'll remember.

(**All** exit.)

Scene 4 🎧

ACT 3
SCENE 4

Olivia's garden. **Olivia** and **Maria** enter.

OLIVIA (*to herself*): I have sent for him.
He says he'll come. How shall I entertain him?
What should I give him? For youth is more often
    bought than begged or borrowed.
I'm speaking too loudly.
(*to Maria*) Where's Malvolio?
He is serious and formal—good qualities
In a servant, considering my situation.
Where is Malvolio?

MARIA: He's coming, madam:
But very strangely. He seems possessed.

OLIVIA: Why, what's the matter? Is he raving?

MARIA: No, madam, he does nothing but smile.
Your ladyship had best have her guard up. I'm
sure the man has lost his wits.

OLIVIA: Go and get him.

(**Maria** leaves.)

I'm as mad as he is—if sad madness
And merry madness are equal.

(**Malvolio** enters.)

Greetings, Malvolio.

MALVOLIO *(smiling broadly)*: Sweet lady, hello.

OLIVIA: Are you smiling? I sent for you because I am sad.

MALVOLIO: Sad, lady? Why so sad?
Haven't you noticed my yellow stockings?
Surely, they should please your eye.

OLIVIA: What's the matter with you?

MALVOLIO: Not full of black thoughts, though my legs are yellow. The commands of the letter will be carried out. We know the sweet Roman handwriting.

OLIVIA: You're acting strangely, Malvolio.

MARIA: How are you, Malvolio?

MALVOLIO: Are you talking to me?
Do nightingales answer crows?

MARIA: Why do you appear before my lady with such ridiculous boldness?

MALVOLIO *(to Olivia)*: *Do not be afraid of greatness*—oh, that was well-written.

OLIVIA: What are you talking about, Malvolio?

MALVOLIO: *Some are born great—*

OLIVIA: What?

MALVOLIO: *Some achieve greatness—*

OLIVIA: What are you saying?

MALVOLIO: *And some have greatness thrust upon them—*

OLIVIA: May heaven cure you!
This is truly midsummer madness!

(A **servant** enters.)

SERVANT: Madam, Count Orsino's young gentleman has returned. It was hard to persuade him to come back. He awaits your lady's pleasure.

OLIVIA: I'll come to him.

(**Servant** exits.)

Good Maria, let this fellow be tended. *(She gestures toward Malvolio.)* Where is my cousin Toby? Some of my people must take special care of him. He must not come to harm for half of my fortune.

(**Olivia** and **Maria** exit.)

MALVOLIO: Oh, ho! It's becoming clearer and clearer. No less a man than Sir Toby to look after me! This goes right along with the letter. As she wrote, she is sending him on purpose, so I can be "openly hostile" to him. It all makes sense. Not one grain of doubt, no obstacle, nothing to come between me and the fulfillment of my hopes! Well, Jove, not I, has done this, and he is to be thanked!

(**Maria** returns with **Sir Toby Belch** and **Fabian**.)

SIR TOBY: Where is he, in the name of all that's holy?

FABIAN: Here he is, here he is. *(to Malvolio)* How are you, sir?

MALVOLIO: Go away. I reject you. Let me enjoy my privacy. Be gone!

MARIA: Look how strangely he's acting! It's as if he's possessed by the devil. Didn't I tell you? Sir Toby, my lady wants you to treat him with care.

MALVOLIO: Ah, ha! Does she really?

SIR TOBY *(to Maria and Fabian)*: Stop! We must deal gently with him. Leave it to me.

(to Malvolio) How do you do, Malvolio? How is everything? Defy the devil! Remember, he's the enemy of mankind.

MALVOLIO: Do you know what you are saying?

MARIA *(to Sir Toby and Fabian)*: Just notice, if you speak ill of the devil, how personally he takes it. Pray God he isn't bewitched.

SIR TOBY: Please, do be quiet. Don't you see how you are annoying him? Leave him to me.

FABIAN: You must use gentleness. Gently! Gently! The devil is violent, and he won't be treated roughly!

SIR TOBY *(to Malvolio)*: Why, hello there, my little bird. How are you, chick?

MALVOLIO: Sir?

SIR TOBY: Yes, duckie, come with me. What, man! It's not wise for a smart fellow like you to play games with Satan. Hang him, that foul creature from the underworld!

MARIA: Get him to say his prayers, good Sir Toby. Get him to pray.

MALVOLIO: My prayers?

MARIA: No, I tell you—he will not hear of godliness.

MALVOLIO: Go and hang yourselves, all of you idle good-for-nothings! I am not like you. You shall know more of me later.

(**Malvolio** exits.)

SIR TOBY: Is it possible?

FABIAN: If this were a stage play, I'd call it unlikely fiction!

SIR TOBY: He has fallen for the joke—hook, line, and sinker, man!

MARIA: But follow him at once, in case the joke goes sour.

SIR TOBY: Here's an idea: We'll put him in a dark room in a straitjacket. My niece already believes that he's mad. We may carry the joke that far, for our pleasure and his pain, until we decide to have mercy on him. But see who's here!

(**Sir Andrew Aguecheek** enters, waving a piece of paper.)

FABIAN: More fun to come!

SIR ANDREW: Here's the challenge. Read it. I promise you there's vinegar and pepper in it.

SIR TOBY: Give it to me. *(He reads.) Youth, whoever you are, you are a scurvy fellow. Don't wonder why I call you that, for I will give you no reason for it.*

FABIAN: A good touch. That keeps you within the law.

SIR TOBY: *You come to the Lady Olivia, and in front of me she treats you kindly. But you lie in your teeth. That's not the reason I'm challenging you. I will waylay you on your way home. If you have the good luck to kill me, you'd be killing me like a rogue and a villain.*

FABIAN: You're still keeping on the right side of the law. Good.

SIR TOBY: *Farewell, and may God have mercy on one of our souls! He may have mercy on mine, so look to yourself. Your friend, as you treat him, and your sworn enemy, Andrew Aguecheek.* If this letter does not move him, his legs cannot. I'll give it to him.

MARIA: Good timing! He is now talking with my lady, and will leave soon.

SIR TOBY: Go, Sir Andrew. Wait for him at the corner of the garden. As soon as you see him, draw your sword and swear horribly. A terrible oath spoken with swaggering self-confidence does more for a man's reputation than an actual swordfight. Go on, now!

SIR ANDREW: You can leave the swearing to me!

(**Sir Andrew** exits.)

SIR TOBY *(to Fabian):* I won't deliver Sir Andrew's letter to the young gentleman. He'll know it was written by a blockhead, and it won't scare him. Instead, I will deliver the challenge by word of mouth. I'll make Aguecheek out to be very brave. The young gentleman will fear his rage, skill, and fury. Both will be so frightened that they will kill each other by exchanging looks!

(**Olivia** and **Viola** enter.)

FABIAN: Here he comes with your niece. Stand aside till he leaves. Then follow him.

SIR TOBY: Meanwhile, I'll think about some horrid message for the challenge.

(**Sir Toby, Fabian,** and **Maria** exit.)

OLIVIA: I have said too much to a heart of stone,
And laid my honor too carelessly on it.
I fear I did wrong, but I was pushed to it
By strong passion.

VIOLA: My master's grief is just as strong as your passion.

OLIVIA *(to Viola)*: Here, wear this locket for me.
It has my picture inside.
Don't refuse it. It has no tongue to annoy you.
And, I beg you, come again tomorrow.
What could you ask of me that I would deny,
As long as it's honorable?

VIOLA: Nothing but this, your true love for my
master.

OLIVIA: How could I honorably give him that
When I have already given it to you?

VIOLA: I will release you.

OLIVIA: Well, come again tomorrow.
Farewell for now.

(**Olivia** exits. **Sir Toby Belch** and **Fabian** return.)

SIR TOBY: Gentleman, God save you.

VIOLA: And you, sir.

SIR TOBY: Whatever weapons you have, get them
ready. I don't know what wrongs you did to
him, but your challenger is as bloodthirsty
as a hunting dog. He's waiting for you by the
garden. Draw your sword and get ready quickly,
for your opponent is fast, skillful, and deadly.

84

VIOLA: You must be mistaken, sir. I am sure no man has any quarrel with me. My memory is free and clear of offense done to anyone.

SIR TOBY: You'll find it otherwise, I assure you. If you value your life, take up your guard. Your opponent has all the gifts of youth, strength, skill, and anger.

ACT 3 SCENE 4

VIOLA: I ask you, sir, who is he?

SIR TOBY: He is a knight, dubbed with a ceremonial sword as he knelt on a carpet. But he is a devil in a private brawl. He's killed three people, and now is so angry that only a death and burial will satisfy him. "Strike first" is his motto, take it or leave it.

VIOLA: I'll go back to the house and ask the lady for protection. I am no fighter.
I've heard of some men who pick fights on purpose just to test their valor.
He must be such a man.

SIR TOBY: Sir, *no*! His anger stems from a very real cause. So you'd better get on with it and give him his satisfaction. You shall not go back to the house unless you cross swords with me. Therefore, go on—or raise your sword against me. You must fight—that's for certain—or stop carrying a weapon.

VIOLA: This is as rude as it is strange! I beg you, tell me how I offended this knight. Surely it's something to do with an oversight, nothing done on purpose.

SIR TOBY: I'll do so. Mister Fabian, stay with this gentleman until I return.

(**Sir Toby** exits.)

VIOLA: Please, sir, do you know of this matter?

FABIAN: I know the knight is incensed against you. He wants it settled in a fight to the death. I don't know any other details.

VIOLA: I beg you, what kind of man is he?

FABIAN: To look at him, you wouldn't see the great promise he shows in action. He is indeed, sir, the most skillful, bloody, and fatal opponent in Illyria. Will you meet him halfway? I'll make your peace with him if I can.

VIOLA: I shall be indebted to you for it.

86

(**They** go. **Viola** is very frightened. **Sir Toby** and **Sir Andrew** return.)

SIR TOBY: Why, man, he's a very devil! I've never seen such a fighter! He strikes as firmly as your feet hit the ground they step on. They say he's been a fencer for the shah of Persia.

SIR ANDREW: A pox on it, I won't duel with him!

SIR TOBY: Yes, but he won't be calmed down. Fabian can hardly hold him back.

SIR ANDREW: Blast it! If I'd thought he was so brave and cunning in fencing, I'd never have challenged him. If he'll let the matter slide, I'll give him my horse, Gray Capilet.

SIR TOBY: I'll see what he says. Stay here, do your best, and this will end without someone's death. *(to himself)* Yes, indeed, I'll take your horse for a ride as well as you!

(**Fabian** and **Viola** enter again.)

SIR TOBY *(to Fabian)*: I have his horse to settle the quarrel. I have persuaded him the youth's a devil.

FABIAN *(to Sir Toby)*: He's as pale as if a bear were chasing him!

SIR TOBY *(to Viola)*: There's no remedy, sir. He'll fight you because he's sworn to. But he's had second thoughts about the quarrel. Now he thinks it was hardly worth talking about. But he means to go ahead with the fight to support his vow. He promises he will not hurt you.

VIOLA *(aside)*: Pray God defend me! I'm tempted to tell them that I'm not a man!

FABIAN: Retreat if you see him furious.

SIR TOBY *(to Sir Andrew)*: Come on, Sir Andrew, there's no remedy. The gentleman will have one bout with you for the sake of his honor. By the rules of dueling, he can't avoid it. But he has promised not to hurt you. Come on. Get going!

SIR ANDREW: Pray God he keeps his promise! *(He draws his sword nervously.)*

VIOLA: I do assure you this is against my will. *(She draws her sword nervously. They both close their eyes and wave their swords around.*

Antonio enters and sees them apparently fighting. He thinks Viola is Sebastian.)

ANTONIO *(to Sir Andrew):* Put up your sword!
  If this young gentleman has offended you,
  I'll answer for him. If you have offended him,
  On his behalf, I defy you. *(Antonio draws his sword expertly.)*

SIR TOBY: You, sir! Who are you?

ANTONIO: One who stands up for his friend!

SIR TOBY: Well, if you're a stand-in, I'm ready for you! *(Sir Toby draws.)*

FABIAN: Stop, Sir Toby! Stop! Here come the officers of the law!

(**Two officers** enter.)

SIR TOBY *(to Antonio):* We'll continue this later.

VIOLA *(to Sir Andrew):* Please, sir, put up your sword, I beg you.

SIR ANDREW *(relieved):* Indeed I will, sir, and I'll keep my promise. Capilet will carry you easily. He responds well to the rein.

FIRST OFFICER *(pointing to Antonio):* This is the man. Do your duty.

SECOND OFFICER: Antonio, I arrest you on order of
Count Orsino.

ANTONIO: You're making a mistake, sir!

FIRST OFFICER: No, sir, no mistake. I know you,
Though you have no sailor's cap on your head.
Take him away. He knows I know him well.

ANTONIO: I'll go quietly. *(to Viola)* This comes
From seeking you. But there's no remedy.
I'll have to answer for it. What will you do,
Now that I must ask for my purse back?
The fact that I cannot help you grieves me
Even more than my own fate.
You look astonished, but be of good cheer.

SECOND OFFICER: Come away, sir.

ANTONIO: I must ask you for that money.

VIOLA: What money, sir?
For the kindness you have just showed me,
And partly because of your present trouble,
I'll lend you some money. I don't have much.
Here, take half of what I have.

ANTONIO *(angrily)*: Will you refuse me now?
Is it possible that what I've done for you
Counts for nothing?

VIOLA: I don't know what you're talking about.
   I've never seen you before in my life.

ANTONIO: Oh, sweet heaven!

SECOND OFFICER: Come, sir, it's time to go.

ANTONIO: Let me speak a little. This youth—
   I snatched him from the jaws of death,
   I helped him with a holy love, and was devoted
      to his very image.

FIRST OFFICER: What's that to us? We're wasting
      time. Let's go.

ANTONIO: But, oh, how wretched an idol he is!
   Sebastian, you have brought
   Shame on your good looks. In nature,
   There's no fault worse than that of the mind.
   Only the unkind can be called deformed.
   Virtue is beauty, but those who are
   Beautiful to look at, although evil inside,
   Are empty boxes overfilled by the devil.

FIRST OFFICER: The man's mad! Come on, sir.

ANTONIO: Lead me on.

(**Officers** and **Antonio** exit.)

VIOLA *(realizing what Antonio has been saying)*:
> Dear brother, could it be true
> That I have now been taken for you?
> He called me "Sebastian." My mirror tells me
> We look exactly alike. I have
> Copied his style for my disguise.
> Oh, if it's true that he is still alive,
> Tempests are kind, and full of love!

(**Viola** exits.)

SIR TOBY: A very dishonorable boy!
> He refused to help his friend in need.
> And as for his cowardice, ask Fabian.

FABIAN: Yes, a coward, a total coward.

SIR ANDREW: By God, I'll chase after him again and
> beat him!

SIR TOBY: Do—beat him up soundly, but don't draw
> your sword.

SIR ANDREW: If I don't—

(**Sir Andrew** exits.)

FABIAN: Come on, let's see what happens.

SIR TOBY: I'll bet that nothing will happen.

(**All** exit.)

ACT 4

Summary

費斯特以為與他在一起的是西薩里奧，
他將西巴斯辛帶回家見奧麗維婭。西巴
斯辛在那被安德魯爵士攻擊，他也誤將西巴斯辛認作是西
薩里奧。但不像他妹妹，西巴斯辛以短刀回擊，接著托比爵
士拔劍相向，卻被奧麗維婭遣走，奧麗維婭將西巴斯辛帶
進屋內。

同時，費斯特穿上教區牧師的服裝，對被關在黑暗屋內的
馬伏里奧胡言亂語。費斯特給馬伏里奧紙和墨水，要他寫
一封信給奧麗維婭以證明他沒有發瘋。在此時，西巴斯辛
被奧麗維婭的情意及美貌所深深吸引，他和奧麗維婭去找
牧師證婚，而想當然地，奧麗維婭以為她所嫁之人是西薩
里奧。

Scene ❶ 🎧17

The street before Olivia's house. **Sebastian** and **Feste** enter.

FESTE: Are you trying to pretend that I wasn't looking for you?

SEBASTIAN: Go away. You are a foolish fellow. Let me be rid of you!

ACT 4
SCENE
1

FESTE: You're keeping this up very well. *(sarcastically)* No, I do not know you. I wasn't sent to you by my lady, who wants to speak with you. And your name is not Cesario. And this isn't even my own nose! Nothing that is so is so!

SEBASTIAN: Please, spout your nonsense somewhere else. You don't know me.

FESTE: Spout my nonsense! What are you talking about? I beg you now, don't be so strange. Tell me what I should say to my lady. Shall I tell her that you are coming?

SEBASTIAN: I beg you, you fool, leave me. Here's some money for you. If you stay longer, I'll give you something worse!

FESTE: Upon my word, you are very generous.
Wise men who give money to fools
Get themselves very well-regarded—
Even 14 years later.

(**Sir Andrew, Sir Toby,** and **Fabian** enter.)

SIR ANDREW *(thinking that Sebastian is Viola)*: Now,
sir, so we meet again! This is for you!
(He strikes Sebastian.)

SEBASTIAN *(striking back)*: And this is for you! And
this! And this! Is everyone here mad?

SIR TOBY: Stop that, sir, or I'll throw your dagger
over the house.

FESTE: I will tell my lady about this right away.
I wouldn't be in your shoes for two cents!

(**Feste** exits.)

SIR TOBY *(holding Sebastian)*: Come on, sir. Stop!

SIR ANDREW: No, let him alone. I'll get at him
another way. I'll take him to court on a battery
charge, if there is any law in Illyria. Though I
struck him first, that doesn't matter.

SEBASTIAN *(to Sir Toby)*: Take your hands off me!

SIR TOBY: Come, sir, I will not let you go.

(Sebastian struggles free.)

SEBASTIAN: Now, what do you have to say?

If you dare to go further, draw your sword!

(Sebastian draws his own sword.)

SIR TOBY: What, what? Well then, I must have an
   ounce or two of your rude blood.

(Sir Toby draws his sword. **Olivia** enters.)

ACT 4
SCENE 1

OLIVIA: Stop, Toby!

SIR TOBY: Madam?

OLIVIA: Must it always be like this? You wretch,
   Fit for the mountains and barbarous caves,
   Where manners were never taught!
   Out of my sight!
   (to Sebastian, thinking he is Viola) Dear
      Cesario,
   Do not be offended.
   (to Sir Toby) You brute! Get out of here!

(**Sir Toby, Sir Andrew,** and **Fabian** exit.)

   (to Sebastian) Gentle friend, let wisdom, not
   Anger, guide your reaction to this
   Rude attack on your peace. Come

To my house and I'll tell you how many
Pointless pranks this brute has had a hand in.
Then you'll be able to smile at this one.
Shame on his soul!
He gave my half of your heart a shock.

SEBASTIAN *(totally puzzled, not knowing Olivia)*:
What is going on? What's the idea?
Am I mad, or is this a dream?
(He sees that Olivia has strong feelings for him.)
If this is a dream, let me stay asleep.

OLIVIA: Please come with me. I wish you would.

SEBASTIAN: Madam, I will.

OLIVIA: Oh, wonderful!

*(**All** exit.)*

Scene 2 18

A room in Olivia's house. **Maria** and **Feste** enter.

MARIA: Now then, put on this gown and this beard.
Make him believe you are Sir Topas, the parson.
Do it quickly while I call Sir Toby.

(**Maria** exits.)

FESTE: Well, I'll put it on to disguise myself.
I wish I were the first man who'd ever practiced
deceit in such a gown!

(**Sir Toby Belch** and **Maria** enter.)

SIR TOBY: God bless you, Master Parson.

FESTE: Good day to you, Sir Toby.

SIR TOBY *(pointing to a door with a small grille to
allow conversation)*: Tend to him, Sir Topas.

FESTE *(in a fake voice)*: Hello there, I say! God's
peace in this prison!

MALVOLIO *(from an inner room, weakly)*: Who's
calling?

FESTE: Sir Topas, the parson, who comes to visit
Malvolio, the lunatic.

MALVOLIO: Sir Topas, Sir Topas, good Sir Topas—go
to my lady.

99

FESTE: Don't you talk about anything but ladies?

SIR TOBY: Well said, Master Parson.

MALVOLIO: Sir Topas, never was a man so wronged.
Please, do not think that I am mad, yet
They keep me here in hideous darkness.

FESTE: Are you saying that place is dark?

MALVOLIO: It is pitch black, Sir Topas!

FESTE: Why, it has bay windows as clear as shutters,
and the high windows toward the south-north
are as bright as ebony. Yet you complain of
darkness?

MALVOLIO: I am not mad, Sir Topas. I tell you this
place is dark.

FESTE: Madman, you are in error. I say there is no
darkness but ignorance,
and you are stuck in it.

MALVOLIO: I say this house is as dark as ignorance,
and I say there was never a man so abused.
I am no more mad than you are! Test me by
asking some searching questions.

FESTE: What did Pythagoras think of wild birds?

MALVOLIO: That the soul of one's grandmother might possibly inhabit a bird.

FESTE: What do you think of that?

MALVOLIO: I think that the soul is noble. I do not agree with Pythagoras.

FESTE: Farewell. Remain in darkness. You must agree with Pythagoras before I will declare you sane. You must be afraid of killing a bird for fear of displacing your grandmother's soul. Farewell.

MALVOLIO: Sir Topas! Sir Topas!

SIR TOBY: My dear Sir Topas!

FESTE *(to Sir Toby)*: I'm a good actor!

MARIA: You could have done this without the disguise. He can't see you.

SIR TOBY: Talk to him in your own voice, and then come and tell me how you find him. *(to Maria)* I wish we were rid of this practical joking. If he can easily be set free, I wish he were. I'm far out of favor with my niece! No, I cannot keep playing this joke. Come to my room by and by.

(**Sir Toby** and **Maria** exit.)

FESTE *(singing in his own voice outside Malvolio's door)*: Hey, Robin, jolly Robin,
Tell me how your lady is.

MALVOLIO: Fool—

FESTE: My lady loves another—Who's calling?

MALVOLIO: Good fool, do me a favor.
Get me a candle, a pen, ink, and paper.
As I am a gentleman, I'll live to show my thanks to you.

FESTE: Master Malvolio!

MALVOLIO: Yes, good fool.

FESTE: Alas, sir. How did you come to be insane?

MALVOLIO: Fool, there was never a man so terribly abused. I am as sane as you are.

FESTE: As sane as I am? Then you are indeed mad, if you are no saner than a fool.

MALVOLIO: They have put me here, kept me in darkness, and sent parsons to me. They do all they can to drive me out of my wits.

FESTE: Take care what you say. The parson is here. *(in his Sir Topas voice)* Malvolio, may the heavens restore your wits! Try to sleep, and stop jabbering nonsense.

MALVOLIO: Sir Topas—

FESTE *(still as Sir Topas)*: Don't talk to him, good fellow. *(his own voice)* Who, I, sir? Not I, sir. God be with you, good Sir Topas. *(Sir Topas again)* Yes, indeed. Amen. *(his own voice)* I will, sir, I will.

MALVOLIO: Fool, fool, fool, I say—

FESTE: Sir, be patient. What do you want? I'm in trouble for speaking to you.

MALVOLIO: Good fool, help me get some light and some paper. I promise you that I'm as sane as any man in Illyria.

FESTE: I wish that you were, sir!

MALVOLIO: By this hand, I am. Give me some ink, paper, and light, and take what I will write to my lady. It shall profit you more than the delivery of any other letter.

FESTE: I will help you. But tell me the truth. Are you really mad, or are you pretending?

ACT 4
SCENE 2

MALVOLIO: Believe me, I am not. I tell the truth.

FESTE: No. I'll never believe a madman till I see his brains. I'll get you light and paper and ink.

MALVOLIO: I'll reward you well. Please go now.

FESTE *(singing)***:** I am gone, sir. But soon, sir, I will be back again.

(**Feste** exits.)

Scene 3 🎧19

Olivia's garden. **Sebastian** enters. He still can't believe he's not dreaming.

SEBASTIAN: This is the air. That's the glorious sun.

This pearl she gave me, I can feel it and see it.

And though I'm filled with wonder, this is

Surely not madness. So where's Antonio?

I could not find him at the Elephant,

Yet he had been there. They told me that

He looked for me all over town.

Now his advice might be worth gold!

This accidental flood of good fortune is

So strange. I argue with my own mind

When it tries to tell me I am not mad.

Or else the lady's mad. But if that were so,

She couldn't rule her house and her servants, or

   manage her affairs

So smoothly and with such confidence.
I don't understand it. But here comes the lady!

(**Olivia** and a **priest** enter.)

OLIVIA: Don't blame me for this haste.
If you mean well, go with me and the priest
Into the nearby chapel. Before him
And under that holy roof, pledge me
Your vows of love in marriage. Then
My jealous and doubtful soul may live at peace.
He shall keep it a secret until you are willing
To make it public. Then we'll have
A celebration in keeping with my rank.
What do you say?

SEBASTIAN: I'll follow this man, and go with you;
And, having made vows, will ever be true.

OLIVIA: Then lead the way, good father.
And may the heavens shine
In blessing of this act of mine!

(**Olivia, Sebastian,** and **priest** exit.)

ACT 5

Summary

在前往拜訪奧麗維婭的路途上，奧西諾和西薩里奧看見執法人員在街上拖行安東尼奧而感到訝異。安東尼奧告訴奧西諾事情原委，並大聲斥責西薩里奧，說他需要他的錢包（他之前將錢包借給西巴斯辛）才能重獲自由。西薩里奧和奧西諾皆對此事感到不解。

接著，奧麗維婭認為西薩里奧就是西巴斯辛，提到他倆不久前才舉辦的婚禮，奧西諾對於西薩里奧的背叛感到憤怒，並威脅要殺了他。然而事態變得更加複雜，西薩里奧向奧西諾傾訴愛意。接著，西巴斯辛上場，他認不出自己的親妹妹，直到兩人彼此質問化解疑惑。

最後，西薩里奧換上女裝，說服奧西諾和西巴斯辛她是女性。雖然奧西諾之前深深愛著奧麗維婭，他此時被薇奧拉吸引。在接近本劇尾聲，馬伏里奧給奧麗維婭看瑪利婭偽造的信，而費比恩解釋這個惡作劇的前因後果。當奧麗維婭下令釋放馬伏里奧後，他氣急敗壞。本劇以雙婚禮作結。

Scene ❶ 🎧

The street before Olivia's house. **Feste** and **Fabian** enter.

FABIAN: Please let me see his letter.

FESTE: Please do not ask to see it.

FABIAN: That's like giving someone a dog and then asking for it back again.

(**Duke, Viola,** and **attendants** enter.)

DUKE: Are you Lady Olivia's men, friends?
Please let your lady know I am here.

FESTE: Gladly, sir.

(**Feste** exits. **Antonio** and **officers** enter.)

VIOLA: Here comes the man who rescued me.

DUKE: I remember that face well,
Even though when I saw it last
It was smeared black in the
Smoke of war. He was captain of
a small vessel
That wasn't worth much. He fought so well
Against the finest ship in our fleet
That even those who suffered great losses

Proclaimed his fame and honor.

(to the officers) What has he done?

FIRST OFFICER: Orsino, this is the Antonio who
Took the *Phoenix* and her cargo from Crete.
He's the one who boarded the *Tiger* when
Your young nephew Titus lost his leg.
We arrested him here in the streets where
He was involved in a private brawl.

VIOLA: He did me a kindness, sir, by drawing
His sword to defend me. After that,
He said some nonsensical things
So I assumed he was mad.

DUKE: Famous pirate! Thief of the high seas!
What foolish boldness brought you here,
At the mercy of your enemies?

ANTONIO: Orsino, noble sir, allow me
To shake off those names you call me.
Antonio was never a thief or pirate—though
There are reasons to be your enemy.
Witchcraft drew me here.
I rescued that most ungrateful boy,
He who is there by your side.

I plucked him from the angry sea.

He was a wreck past hope. I gave him his life

And added to it my love. For his sake,

I exposed myself to danger in this town.

I drew my sword to defend him from attack.

When I was arrested, his false cunning led him

To deny our friendship to my face.

In the time it takes to blink, he'd turned into

Someone who'd not seen me for 20 years.

He denied me my own purse, which

I'd given him not half an hour before.

VIOLA *(astonished)*: How can this be?

DUKE *(to the officers)*: When did he arrive here?

ANTONIO *(answering for himself)*: Today, my lord.

For three months before this, we'd been

Together day and night, without a break

Of so much as a minute.

(**Olivia** and **attendants** enter.)

DUKE: Here comes the countess.

Now heaven walks on earth!

(to Antonio) As for you, you speak madness.

For the past three months this youth

Has been my servant. But more of that later.
(to the officers) Take him to one side.

OLIVIA: What does my lord wish—other than
What he cannot have—that Olivia can supply?
*(She sees Viola, mistaking her for her new
husband.)* Cesario, you are not keeping your
promise.

VIOLA *(not understanding)*: Madam?

DUKE: Gracious Olivia—

OLIVIA: What do you say, Cesario? *(seeing the duke
start to speak, she stops him)*
Please, my lord—

VIOLA: My lord wishes to speak.
Duty demands that I remain silent.

OLIVIA: If it's your same old tune, my lord,
It sounds to me like howling.

DUKE: Still so cruel?

OLIVIA: Still so consistent, my lord.

DUKE: Consistently *perverse*! You rude lady,
At whose ungrateful altars my soul
Has offered the most faithful prayers!
What shall I do?

OLIVIA: Whatever pleases you, my lord.

DUKE: Listen to this. Since you refuse my love,
And because I think I know
What has replaced me in your favor,
Remain the coldhearted tyrant you are!
But your darling, whom I know you love—
I swear by heaven that I will tear him out of
That cruel eye of yours where he sits crowned
Instead of me. *(to Viola)* Come with me, boy.
My thoughts are full of mischief.
I'll sacrifice the lamb I love *(he means Viola)*,
To spite the raven's heart that lives
Within a dove *(he means Olivia)*.

VIOLA: And I would willingly and happily
Die a thousand deaths,
If that would give you peace of mind.

*(The **duke** and **Viola** start to go.)*

OLIVIA: Where is Cesario going?

VIOLA: After the man I love—
More than I love my eyes, more than my life,
More than I shall ever love a wife.
If I am lying, you gods above
Punish me for tainting my love!

OLIVIA *(thinking she is being jilted)*: Alas, how I have
   been misled!

VIOLA: Who has misled you? Who does you wrong?

OLIVIA: Have you forgotten? Has it been so long?
   Call the holy father.

(An **attendant** exits.)

DUKE *(to Viola)*: Come away!

OLIVIA: Where, my lord? Cesario, husband, stay.

DUKE: Husband?

OLIVIA: Yes, husband. Can he deny it?

DUKE *(to Viola)*: Her husband, sir?

VIOLA: No, my lord, not I!

OLIVIA: Alas, it is cowardly to deny your
   Own identity. Fear not, Cesario.
   Take possession of your good fortune.
   Be what you know you are!
   Then you are as great as him you fear.

(The **priest** enters.)

   Welcome, Father! Father, I ask you
   To tell all you know about what
   Happened between this youth and me.

PRIEST: A contract eternally binding of love,
Confirmed by holding hands, and
Proven with a holy kiss,
Strengthened by the exchange of your rings.
All the ceremony of this agreement was sealed
By me as priest and witness.
This took place only two hours ago.

DUKE *(to Viola)*: Oh, you lying cub!
What will you be like by the time you're gray?
Or will your craftiness grow so fast
That you'll trip yourself up?
Farewell, then. But be sure our paths
Never cross in the future.

VIOLA: My lord, I swear—

OLIVIA: Oh, do not swear!
Keep some of your honor, despite your fear.

(**Sir Andrew Aguecheek** enters, his head injured.)

SIR ANDREW: For the love of God, a surgeon!
Send one to Sir Toby right away.

OLIVIA: What's the matter?

SIR ANDREW: He has split my skull and given
Sir Toby a cut head, too. Help us!
I'd give a hundred dollars to go home.

OLIVIA: Who has done this, Sir Andrew?

SIR ANDREW: The count's gentleman, that Cesario fellow. We thought he was a coward, but he's the devil himself!

DUKE: My man Cesario?

SIR ANDREW *(noticing Viola for the first time)*: By God, here he is! *(to Viola)* You broke my head for nothing! What I did, Sir Toby made me do.

VIOLA: Why speak to me? I never hurt you.
You drew your sword on me without cause,
But I was polite to you and didn't hurt you.

SIR ANDREW: If a bloody head is a hurt, you have hurt me! I guess you think a bloody head is nothing!

*(**Sir Toby Belch** enters, drunk, led by **Feste**.)*

Here comes Sir Toby, limping. He'll have something to say. If he hadn't been drunk, he'd have fixed you better than he did!

DUKE: Well now, gentleman! How are you?

FESTE: Oh, he's drunk, since an hour ago. His eyes were glassy at eight this morning.

SIR TOBY *(staggering)*: Then he's a rogue and a
staggering fool! I hate a drunken rogue!

OLIVIA: Take him away. Who has done this to them?

SIR ANDREW: I'll help you, Sir Toby, because our
wounds can be dressed together.

OLIVIA: Get him to bed, and see to his injuries.

(**Feste, Sir Toby,** and **Sir Andrew** exit. **Sebastian**
enters.)

SEBASTIAN: I'm sorry, madam, for hurting him.
But had he been my own brother,
I could have done no less to defend myself.
You're looking at me strangely.
I can tell I have offended you. Forgive me,
Sweet one, on the strength of the vows
We made to each other so recently.

ACT **5**
SCENE
1

DUKE *(totally amazed)*: One face. One voice.
One style of dress. And two persons!

SEBASTIAN *(seeing his old friend)*: Antonio!
Oh, my dear Antonio!
How agonizing the hours have been
Since losing you!

ANTONIO: Are you—Sebastian?

SEBASTIAN: Do you doubt it, Antonio?

ANTONIO: How have you divided yourself?
An apple, cut in two, is not more twin
Than these two creatures. Which is Sebastian?

OLIVIA: Amazing!

SEBASTIAN *(looking at Viola):* Do I stand there?
I never had a brother . . . nor do I have
The divine gift of being here and everywhere.
I had a sister, whom the cruel sea has taken.

(to Viola) What relation are you to me?
What's your country? What's your name?
Who were your parents?

VIOLA: I'm from Messaline. Sebastian was
My father's name, and my brother's, too.
He was dressed like this when he drowned.
If spirits can take on both the body
And the clothes, you've come to frighten us.

SEBASTIAN: I am a spirit indeed—but of the
Material world into which I was born.
If you were a woman, since all else fits,
I'd shed my tears and say,
"Welcome, welcome, drowned Viola!"

VIOLA: My father had a mole upon his brow.

SEBASTIAN: And so had mine.

VIOLA: And died on my thirteenth birthday.

SEBASTIAN: The memory is vivid in my soul.
He finished his mortal life on the day
My sister and I turned thirteen.

VIOLA: If nothing prevents our happiness
But these masculine clothes I'm wearing,
Let me prove that I am Viola. Come meet

A captain in this town. My own clothes
Are at his house. Through his kind help,
I was saved, to serve this noble count.
All my life since then has been devoted
To this lady and this lord.

DUKE: Don't be alarmed—he's of noble blood.
If this is true, and it certainly seems to be,
I shall have a share in this most fortunate
Of shipwrecks. *(to Viola)* Boy, you have said
To me a thousand times that you would never
Love a woman as much as you love me.

VIOLA: And all those sayings I will swear again!

DUKE: Give me your hand,
And let me see you in your woman's clothes.

VIOLA: The captain who first brought me ashore
Has my clothes. He's under arrest over some
Legal matter which Malvolio has started.

OLIVIA: He will set him free. Fetch Malvolio here.
But, alas—I've just remembered. They say
He's mentally disturbed, poor gentleman.

(**Feste** enters again, with a letter, followed by **Fabian**.)

(to Feste) How is he, fellow?

FESTE: Truly, madam, he's doing as well
As any man in his situation can do.
He has written a letter to you.

OLIVIA: Open it, and read it.

FESTE *(using a weird sort of voice)*: *By the Lord,
madam—*

OLIVIA: What, are you mad, too?

FESTE: No, madam, I'm only reading madness.
If your ladyship wants it spoken as it should be,
you must allow for a special voice.

OLIVIA: Please, read it as though you are sane.

FESTE: Yes, my lady. *(reading) By the Lord, madam,
you do me wrong, and the world shall know it.
Though you have sent me into a dark room and
put me in charge of your drunken cousin, I am
as sane as your ladyship. I have your own letter
that persuaded me to act as I did. This will
defend me and put you to shame. Think what
you like about me. I should be more polite, but I
speak from a sense of injustice.*
—The Madly Used Malvolio

OLIVIA: Did he write this?

FESTE: Yes, madam.

DUKE: This doesn't sound like madness.

OLIVIA: Set him free, Fabian, and bring him here.
(**Fabian** exits.)

My lord, I hope you'll accept me as a
Sister-in-law rather than a wife.
If you agree, the ceremonies will be
The same day, here at my house,
And at my expense.

DUKE: Madam, I happily accept your offer.
(to Viola) Your master releases you. And,
For your service to him—so unfeminine and
So far beneath your gentle upbringing—
And since you called me "master" for so long,
Here is my hand. *(Viola takes it.)*
From this time, you shall be your master's wife.

OLIVIA *(to Viola)*: A sister—that's what you are!
(**Fabian** enters again, with **Malvolio.**)

DUKE: Is this the madman?

OLIVIA: Yes, my lord. How are you, Malvolio?

MALVOLIO: Madam, you have wronged me.
Wronged me terribly.

OLIVIA: Have I, Malvolio? Surely not.

MALVOLIO: Lady, you have. Please read this letter.
(He hands her Maria's forgery.)
You cannot deny this is your seal.
Well, admit it then,
And tell me, honestly, why you told me to
Come smiling and wearing yellow stockings.
Why did you tell me to frown at Sir Toby
And the servants? And why, after I did all this,
Did you have me kept in a dark house,
Visited by the priest, and made the biggest
Fool and idiot ever tricked? Tell me why.

OLIVIA: Alas, Malvolio, this is not my writing,
Though, I confess, it's very close.
Without question, it's Maria's handwriting.
And now that I think of it, it was Maria who
First told me you were mad. Then you came in
Smiling, acting as suggested in this letter.
This joke has been played on you very cleverly.

When we know who did it, you shall
Be both judge and jury in your own case.

FABIAN: Dear madam, let me speak.
May no quarrel or future brawl spoil
The pleasure of this present time, which
Has astonished me. In hope that it won't,
I confess most freely that Toby and I
Played this trick on Malvolio because
We didn't like his proud and rude manner.
Maria wrote this letter under Sir Toby's
   orders,
And he has married her in exchange.
How the trick was mischievously carried out
May cause laughter rather than desire
For revenge, especially if the grievances
On both sides are fairly weighed.

OLIVIA *(to Malvolio)*: Alas, you poor man!
How they've made a fool of you!

MALVOLIO: I'll have my revenge on all of you!

(**Malvolio** exits.)

OLIVIA: He has been terribly wronged.

DUKE *(to Fabian):* Go after him! Make your peace.
    He hasn't told us about the captain yet.
    When that is sorted out, and the
      time is right,
    We'll all be united in holy wedlock.
    (to Olivia) Meantime, sweet sister,
    We'll stay here.
    (to Viola) Cesario—for so I'll call you
    While you're dressed like a man—come.
    (He offers her his arm.)
    When in other garments you are seen,
    You'll be Orsino's wife, and his heart's queen.

(**All** exit.)

·中文翻譯

英文內文 P. 004

背景

伊利里亞公爵奧西諾深愛著奧麗維婭女伯爵——但是她不願與他有絲毫瓜葛。奧西諾差遣他的隨從西薩里奧（偽裝的薇奧拉，愛上了他）代他去求愛，不料奧麗維婭竟愛上了西薩里奧。

薇奧拉的孿生兄弟西巴斯辛（她以為他已在船難中不幸溺斃）來到了伊利里亞，奧麗維婭誤將西巴斯辛認作他偽裝的姊妹，而西巴斯辛也愛上了奧麗維婭。後續的情況變得更複雜，最後才揭露了所有人的身分，故事也有了圓滿的結局。

人物介紹

P. 005

奧西諾：伊利里亞公爵
西巴斯辛：一位年輕的紳士，薇奧拉的兄弟
安東尼奧：一位航海船長，西巴斯辛的朋友
一位航海船長：薇奧拉的朋友
凡倫丁與丘里奧：兩位紳士
托比·培爾契爵士：奧麗維婭的叔父
安德魯·艾古契克爵士：托比爵士的朋友
奧麗維婭：一位富有的女伯爵

薇奧拉：西巴斯辛的妹妹；後來偽裝成西薩里奧
瑪利婭：奧麗維婭的侍女
馬伏里奧：奧麗維婭的管家
費比恩：奧麗維婭的僕人
費斯特：奧麗維婭的弄臣
貴族諸公、一位牧師、水手們、執法人員們、樂師們與其他人

第一幕

● 第一場─────────────────────P. 007

（在伊利里亞，公爵宮殿的一個大房間；公爵、丘里奧與貴族諸公上；
樂師們演奏。）

公爵：倘若音樂是愛情的食糧，繼續演奏吧，給我再多也不
嫌多。我狼吞虎嚥，食慾或能衰減，順勢死去。（聆聽半
晌。）夠了！莫再演奏！如今已不似從前那般悅耳了。喔，
愛情的精靈！你是多麼地活躍和清新！儘管有如海水一樣
深，再珍貴之物來到你面前，多少都要失色，即便只是須
臾！愛情如此形形色色，其奢華程度無可比擬。

丘里奧：你要去狩獵嗎，閣下？

公爵：狩獵什麼，丘里奧？

丘里奧：雄鹿。

公爵（將他的手按在心上）：哎呀，這正是我在做的事。當我這
雙眼睛初見奧麗維婭之際，我便認為她淨化了空氣；在那
個當下，我即化成了一隻雄鹿，而我的慾望有如兇猛殘酷
的獵犬一般追逐我至今。

（凡倫丁上。）

公爵：如何？她捎來什麼消息？

凡倫丁：閣下，我並未受邀入內。她透過女僕的答覆是這樣的：未來的七個寒暑，即便是太陽也見不到她的臉龐；她將如修女一般戴著面紗，在她的閨房裡終日以淚洗面，以此為她已故的兄長守喪，懷著哀傷的心情時時緬懷她兄長的關愛。

公爵：喔，她的心腸如此地柔軟，單只為了兄長就要這般償還情感的債！當丘比特的箭射中她的心坎之時，她要如何去愛？領我前去百花盛開的園圃吧！在樹蔭之下，相思情意更濃。

（全體下。）

● 第二場 P. 009

（海濱；薇奧拉、船長與水手們上。）

薇奧拉：此乃何國，朋友們？

船長：此為伊利里亞，小姐。

薇奧拉：我何以來到伊利里亞？我的兄弟已上了天堂，但是他或許並未溺斃，你意下如何？

船長：你是幸運獲救。

薇奧拉：喔，我可憐的兄弟！或許他亦已獲救。

船長：是的，小姐，在我們的船出現了裂痕之後，我們緊抓住漂浮的船身時，我看到你的兄弟將自己縛於桅杆之上。在我視力可及的範圍內，他始終在海浪中載浮載沉。

薇奧拉（拿錢給他）：憑你這番話，我該給你黃金。我僥倖逃過此劫，即存著希望他亦躲過劫難。你對此國是否熟悉？

船長：是的，我在此出生長大。

薇奧拉：此地由何人統治？

船長：一位名為奧西諾的尊貴公爵。

薇奧拉：奧西諾！我聽家父提起過他，當年他還單身。

船長：他至今仍是單身──至少直到最近仍是。一個月前在我出海之時，我聽聞了他向美麗的奧麗維婭求愛的謠傳。

薇奧拉：她是何人？

船長：一位品德高尚的女子，一年前過世的一位伯爵之女。他將她交予他兒子、她兄長保護，孰料她兄長未幾即英年早逝。據說為了回報他的恩情，她已然回絕任何男子的陪伴，甚至不願見到男人！

薇奧拉：但願我能服侍那位女子，在更瞭解自己的情況之前，亦能躲避眾人的目光。

船長：這可非易事。她不會考慮任何請求──即便公爵亦被拒於門外。

薇奧拉：你似乎是個好人，船長，你是否願意──我會付你豐厚的酬勞──幫助我偽裝身分？我想服侍這位公爵，你可以當我是個年輕男子引薦予他，保證酬勞必使你值回票價。我會唱歌，亦能用許多形式的音樂與他溝通，因此我必會是吸引他的雇工。無論如何，日久見人心，但請你保持緘默，如此可好？

船長：倘若我未能保持緘默，但願我的雙眼全盲！

薇奧拉：謝謝你。（她示意。）你先請……

（他們下。）

129

（在奧麗維婭家中的一個房間；托比‧培爾契爵士與瑪利婭上。）

托比爵士：我的姪女此舉究竟是何意，竟是如此面對她兄長之死？我相信擔憂是無益於她的健康。

瑪利婭：是的，托比爵士，你今晚務必要提早返家，你的姪女不喜歡你晚歸，而你飲酒過度亦會傷身；我昨日才聽聞小姐提及此事。她還提到一位愚蠢的騎士，是你某天晚上帶回來意欲追求她的。

托比爵士：是何人？可是安德魯‧艾古契克爵士？他在伊利里亞可是無人出其左右的。

瑪利婭：此言何意？

托比爵士：哎呀，他富可敵國！

瑪利婭：或許吧，但是他的錢只能維持一年。他不但是個傻瓜，還揮金如土。

托比爵士：你這番話也未免太無禮！他會彈奏小提琴，還會說三、四種語言；他可謂是天生才華橫溢啊。

瑪利婭：確實如此，他是天生的蠢才！除了愚蠢之外，他還好爭辯。所幸他也有懦弱的天分，削減了他對爭辯的熱情，否則他恐怕早已被葬入墳墓──此乃學識淵博者所言！

托比爵士：說出此話者皆為惡徒！他們是何人？

瑪利婭：說他每晚皆與你共飲至爛醉之人。

托比爵士：我是飲酒祝福我姪女健康！怎麼，小姑娘？說曹操，曹操就到──安德魯‧艾古契克爵士來了。

（安德魯‧艾古契克爵士上。）

安德魯爵士：托比‧培爾契爵士！你好！

托比爵士（擁抱他）：親愛的安德魯爵士！

安德魯爵士（對瑪利婭）：祝福你，美麗的潑婦。（他以為這是恭維之語。）

瑪利婭（忍住不發笑）：你也是，先生。

托比爵士：向她搭訕，安德魯爵士，向她搭訕。

安德魯爵士（不解「搭訕」為何意）：這是何意？

托比爵士（眨眼）：我姪女的貼身侍女！

安德魯爵士（誤解）：親愛的搭訕小姐，我意欲更進一步認識你。

瑪利婭：我名叫瑪麗，先生。

安德魯爵士：親愛的瑪麗‧搭訕小姐──

托比爵士（打斷他的話）：你誤解了，騎士，「搭訕」意指親近她、向她示好、與她調情、引她注意。

安德魯爵士：哎呀，我在此場合是不會與她打交道的。此一詞可是這個意思？

瑪利婭（轉身離開）：再見，兩位紳士。

（瑪利婭下。）

托比爵士：喔，騎士！你需要喝杯酒。我幾時見過你如此沒出息了？怎麼了，我親愛的騎士？

安德魯爵士：托比爵士，你姪女不肯見我。即使她見了我，十之八九她是不會想與我有半點瓜葛的。住在這鄰近的公爵，恰巧也在追求她。

托比爵士：她是不會與那位公爵往來的。她不會嫁給高於自身的對象──不論財富、年齡或智力。聽說她還為此發過誓。胡扯！你還是有機會能追求到她！

安德魯爵士：我會再多留一個月，畢竟我是個玩心未泯之人；我喜歡化妝宴會和舞會，有時兩者合一更好。

托比爵士：你很擅長跳舞嗎，騎士？

安德魯爵士：如同伊利里亞的任何人一般擅長，只要他的位階比我低。但是我比不上經驗豐富之人。

托比爵士：你可熟悉侶爾舞，騎士？

安德魯爵士：我想我能跳得和任何人一般好！（他示範，舞步拙劣。）

托比爵士（假意誇讚他）：你何以一直隱藏才華？此般天分何以孤芳自賞？像畫作一般，藏久了亦可能佈滿灰塵。你何不跳著侶爾舞一路前往教堂，再跳著高地福靈舞回家？換作是我，我會用吉格舞步走路。你在想什麼？在這世上有必要藏起美德嗎？瞧瞧你的腿部線條如此優美，想必是長期跳舞使然。

安德魯爵士（自誇）：是的，我的腿很結實──穿上橘紅色的長襪著實好看。我們要去飲酒作樂嗎？

托比爵士：那是當然！讓我見識你的舞步。（安德魯爵士開始跳舞。）熱情點！（安德魯爵士竭盡他的全力。）哈哈！好極了！

（他們下。）

●第四場 ———————————————— P. 017

（在公爵宮殿中的一個房間；凡倫丁與薇奧拉上，後者打扮成一位年輕人，改名為西薩里奧。）

凡倫丁：倘若公爵繼續看重你，西薩里奧，你未幾即可能步步高升。他認識你才三日就已經與你熟稔了。

薇奧拉：謝謝你。公爵來了。

（公爵、丘里奧與侍從們上。）

公爵：可有人見到西薩里奧？

薇奧拉：隨時聽候差遣，閣下。

公爵（對他的侍從們）：暫且回避。（對薇奧拉：）西薩里奧，你什麼都知道了，我已對你坦白我心中的秘密。所以年輕人，請你去找她，站在她的門口，告訴他們在你受邀入內之前，你的雙腳就像生了根似地一動也不動。

薇奧拉：好的，我尊貴的閣下。倘若她如旁人所說地沉浸在悲傷之中，她是說什麼也不會讓我入內的。

公爵：莫要接受她的拒絕！

薇奧拉：假設我真能與她面談，閣下，我該怎麼做？

公爵：喔，對她傾訴我的情衷；提及我對她的深切愛意，使她驚訝。你若能與她面談就太好了；相較於年長的信差，她理應會聽你這年輕人說話。

薇奧拉：我倒不以為然，閣下。

公爵：親愛的孩子，相信吧，此事交託予你最是合適。你好好表現，我會分給你部分的財產作為獎賞。

薇奧拉：我會竭盡全力去追求你那位小姐。（竊語：）此事難如登天！不論我追求何人，我其實一心只想嫁給你！

（在奧麗維婭家中的一個房間；瑪利婭與費斯特上。）

瑪利婭：告訴我你去了何處，否則我不會開口為你編造任何藉口。你去了那麼久，我家小姐會解雇你的。

費斯特：隨她去吧！至少時已入夏，我流落街頭不至於凍死。

瑪利婭：我家小姐來了，你最好自己想個好藉口。

（瑪利婭下。）

費斯特（彷彿在禱告）：喔，機智啊，倘若你願意，請幫助我機智應變。自以為機智的弄臣們，經常到頭來都被證明是傻子。既然我自知並不機智，或許我能成為睿智之人。那句俗話是怎麼說的？「寧可當個機智的傻子，也不要當個愚笨的才子。」（奧麗維婭與馬伏里奧上，侍從們尾隨而上。）願上蒼保佑你，小姐！

奧麗維婭（用厭煩的手勢）：將這傻子帶走。

費斯特（對侍從們）：你們這些傢伙沒聽見嗎？將小姐帶走！

奧麗維婭：莫要胡說八道，你的機智毫不幽默，我已經受夠你了，況且你愈來愈不誠實。

費斯特：小姐，飲酒和忠告能治癒兩個缺陷。給這個不幽默的傻子喝杯酒，未幾這傻子即能變得幽默。吩咐不誠實之人改正自己，倘若他做到了，那他便不再不誠實；倘若他無法改正自己，就找個廉價的裁縫師來修補他。凡是修補過的皆是補綴；出了錯的美德是用罪惡來補綴，有罪而能改之則是以美德來補綴。倘若這簡單的邏輯適用於你，那就好；倘若不能，吾人又能如何處置？（對侍從們：）小姐要你們將這傻子帶走，所以我再說一遍，將她帶走吧。

奧麗維婭：先生，我是請他們將你帶走。

費斯特：此乃最嚴重的謬誤！小姐，「身穿袈裟之人未必皆為
僧侶」；換言之，莫要被我的弄臣打扮給欺騙了。好小姐，
讓我證明你才是傻子吧。

奧麗維婭：你能證明嗎？

費斯特：易如反掌，好小姐。

奧麗維婭：那你就證明吧。

費斯特：我必須請教你幾個問題才能證明，小姐。

奧麗維婭：先生，我沒有更好的事可以做，只好奉陪你了。

費斯特：小姐，你何以悲嘆？

奧麗維婭：好傻子，因我兄長之死。

費斯特：我認為他的靈魂在地獄裡，小姐。

奧麗維婭：我知道他的靈魂在天堂裡，傻子。

費斯特：那你更傻啊，小姐，竟然因你兄長的靈魂在天堂裡
而悲嘆。（**對侍從們**：）將這傻子帶走，諸位。

奧麗維婭（**對馬伏里奧**）：你對這傻子有何看法，馬伏里奧？他
莫不是有進步了？

馬伏里奧：是的，他會繼續進步，直到他承受臨終之苦。年
老會使智慧衰退，亦會使得傻子更傻。

費斯特：但願上蒼使你快速變老，先生，讓你變得更加愚蠢！
托比爵士會發誓我並不機智，但是他不會毫不遲疑地發誓
你不是個傻子。

奧麗維婭：對此你怎麼說，馬伏里奧？

馬伏里奧：我很訝異小姐你竟然喜歡這如此腦袋空空的惡
徒。

奧麗維婭：喔，你太嚴肅地看待自己了，而且你的判斷力不
佳。善良之人會包容他人的缺陷。

（瑪利婭再上。）

瑪利婭：小姐，門口有位年輕紳士求見你。

奧麗維婭：可是奧西諾公爵派來的？

瑪利婭：我不知道，小姐。他是個長相俊美的年輕人，還帶了幾名侍從。

奧麗維婭：是我們家的誰要他等候？

瑪利婭：是托比爵士，小姐，你的親眷。

奧麗維婭：去請托比爵士離開，他成天瘋言瘋語的，真是可恥！（*瑪利婭下。*）你去吧，馬伏里奧。倘若他是為公爵傳達口信，就跟他說我病了，或是不在家；隨你怎麼說，只消擺脫他便可。（*馬伏里奧下。奧麗維婭轉向費斯特。*）如今你該明白了，先生，旁人有多不喜歡你的玩笑。

費斯特：你為我們這些弄臣美言了，小姐，彷彿你的長子即是個傻子似的。願上蒼在他的頭骨之內塞進腦子——因你不甚聰明的一位親戚來了。

（*托比‧培爾契爵士上。*）

奧麗維婭：我以名譽擔保，他已是半醉！（*對托比爵士：*）在門口等候的是怎樣的人，叔父？

托比爵士：一位紳士。

奧麗維婭：一位紳士？什麼紳士？

托比爵士：有位紳士來了。（*他大聲地打嗝。*）都怪這些醃鯡魚！（*對費斯特：*）你好啊，傻子！

費斯特：親愛的托比爵士！

奧麗維婭：叔父，叔父，你何以這麼早就如此精神不濟、昏昏欲睡？

托比爵士（*誤解*）：魂昏慾仙！我最瞧不起縱慾之人了。有個人來到門口。

奧麗維婭：是的，他是怎樣的人？

托比爵士：就如他所願地讓他當個魔鬼吧，我不在乎，於我皆無異。

（托比爵士下。）

奧麗維婭：喝醉的人是怎樣，傻子？

費斯特：如同溺水的人、傻子和瘋子一般。多喝個一杯會使他變得愚蠢，多喝個兩杯會使他發瘋，多喝個三杯會溺死他。

奧麗維婭：去找驗屍官過來，讓他帶走我的叔父，因他已是三級醉酒狀態。他溺死了，快去照看他。

費斯特：他只達發瘋的階段，小姐。傻子這就去照看那個瘋子。

（費斯特下，馬伏里奧再上。）

馬伏里奧：小姐，門口那位年輕人發誓他非與你面談不可。我推說你病了，他說他早已知曉，因此他才要前來與你相談。我又推說你已睡下，他宣稱他亦早已知曉，因此他才要前來與你相談。我該如何回覆他，小姐？不管我怎麼說，他都能見招拆招。

奧麗維婭：就說他不能與我面談。

馬伏里奧：我已如是告訴他，他說他會像旗桿似地在你的門口，或是像板凳似地架著不動——但是他非與你面談不可。

奧麗維婭：他是怎樣的人？

馬伏里奧：哎呀，在人類之中……

奧麗維婭：怎樣的人？

馬伏里奧：非常無禮。不管你是否願意，他都要與你面談。

奧麗維婭：他的相貌如何，年方幾何？

馬伏里奧：年紀不夠稱得上是個男人，稱他是個男孩卻又不夠年輕。他的相貌非常俊美。

奧麗維婭：讓他進來吧。傳我的侍女前來。

馬伏里奧：侍女！我家小姐叫你。

（馬伏里奧下，瑪利婭再上。）

奧麗維婭：將我的頭紗拿來，蓋在我的臉上。我們再聽聽奧西諾的信差要説些什麼。

（薇奧拉上，打扮成西薩里奧。）

薇奧拉：府上的女主人是哪一位？

奧麗維婭：由我來代她發言。有何貴幹？

薇奧拉（開始她預備好的說詞）：最是容光煥發、姿態優雅又貌若天仙……（中斷。）拜託，請告訴我這位是否為府上的女主人，因我未曾見過她，我不想浪費唇舌；這講稿除了寫得很好之外，我亦費盡功夫熟記於心。（瑪利婭忍不住發笑。）請你莫要笑我，我可是非常敏感。

奧麗維婭：你是打哪兒來的，先生？

薇奧拉：我只能説出預先熟記的話，此一問題不在我的劇本中。高尚的小姐，請讓我略微確知你是府上的女主人。

奧麗維婭：你是個演員嗎？

薇奧拉：不是，但是我發誓我並非如外表看來這樣。你可是府上的女主人？

奧麗維婭：是的。

薇奧拉：那我就繼續照稿稱讚你吧。語罷，我便會説出此次口信的重點。

奧麗維婭：説重點吧，毋需再讚美。

薇奧拉：我好不容易才熟記於心，內容很詩意。

奧麗維婭：那就更有可能是假的了，請你莫要再説。我聽聞你厚顏駐足於我家門口，我讓你進來乃是出於對你的好奇，而非意欲聽你説話。倘若你生氣了，那就請回吧；倘

　　若你神志清楚，請長話短說，我沒心情和你如此愚謬地對
　　話。你有什麼話就說吧。

薇奧拉：我是個信差。

奧麗維婭：是啊，你如此拘泥於複雜的形式，想必你有可怕
　　的口信要傳達。是什麼事？

薇奧拉：我只能說給你一人聽。我既非來宣戰，亦非來催討
　　稅金；我手中握著橄欖枝，我說的話充滿和平，無意爭辯。

奧麗維婭：但你起初很是無禮。你是何人？有何貴幹？

薇奧拉：我無禮乃因我被無禮地對待。至於我是何人和有何
　　貴幹，則是如童貞一般的秘密；聽在你耳裡是神聖的，聽
　　在他人耳裡則是褻瀆。

奧麗維婭（對瑪利婭）：你先退下吧，我來聽聽這所謂的「神
　　聖」。

（瑪利婭下。）

薇奧拉：最甜美的小姐……

奧麗維婭：你這番說詞是從何而來？

薇奧拉：來自奧西諾的心中。

奧麗維婭：他的心中？在他內心的哪一章節？

薇奧拉：按照你的方式來回答：是他內心的第一章節。

奧麗維婭：喔，我已經讀過了，那是異端邪說。你還有其他的
　　話要說嗎？

薇奧拉：好小姐，讓我看看你的臉。

奧麗維婭：是你家主人要你與我的臉協商嗎？那就拉開布
　　幕，讓你看看這幅畫吧。（她掀開面紗。）畫得很像吧？

薇奧拉：畫得好極了，倘若這一切皆是上帝之作。

奧麗維婭：這是受保護的，先生，能耐得住風吹日曬和雨淋。

薇奧拉：此乃混合得宜之美貌，由大自然親手調和的色彩。

小姐，倘若你將帶著這些天賦踏進墳墓，在人間未能留下複製品，那你就是這世上最殘酷的女人了。

奧麗維婭：喔，先生，我不會如此冷血無情。我會公布我美貌的不同清單，然後逐一清點，每個細節皆如我所願地貼上標籤。物件：兩片櫻紅的嘴唇。物件：兩隻灰色的眼睛，附有眼瞼。物件：一個脖子和一個下巴等等。你是受命來此讚美我的嗎？

薇奧拉：我明白你是怎麼了！你太驕傲了，但即便你是魔鬼，你仍然美麗！我家主人深愛著你。

奧麗維婭：他是如何愛我？

薇奧拉：極其仰慕，相思成淚，痛苦的呻吟聲震響了愛意，還有烈火一般的嘆息。

奧麗維婭：你家主人知道我的心意，我無法愛他，但是我相信他才德兼備，我知道他高尚、富有又年輕；他受人敬重、愛好自由、有教養又勇敢，亦有人說他寬大為懷，但我就是無法愛他。他應該早已知曉我的答案。

薇奧拉：倘若我愛你如我家主人一般，吃盡苦頭又痛苦不堪，我不會接受你這樣的回答，我亦不可能明白。

奧麗維婭：哎呀，那你會如何回應？

薇奧拉：我會在你的門口搭建一座小屋，不時登門探望我心愛之人；我會編寫真摯的單戀情歌，即便在夜深人靜時也要高聲吟唱；我會向著餘音繚繞的山巒呼喊你的名字，使「奧麗維婭！」的回音響徹雲霄。喔，你不可能活在這世上卻不同情我。

奧麗維婭：以你的例子，你或許能成功。你是何背景來歷？

薇奧拉：比我目前的情況更好，我是個紳士。

奧麗維婭：去回覆你家主人，我無法愛他，請他莫要再來傳遞口信——除非恰巧是你再來告訴我他的回應。再見了，謝謝你的奔波和辛勞。（她給了薇奧拉一些錢。）替我花掉這些錢。

薇奧拉（拒絕）：我並非受雇的信差，小姐。你的錢留著，欠缺獎賞的是我家主人，而不是我。但願你所愛之人擁有一顆鐵石心腸，讓你的熱情和我家主人一樣，被人輕蔑以待！再會了，你這殘酷的美人！

（薇奧拉下。）

奧麗維婭：你是何背景來歷？「比我目前的情況更好，我是個紳士。」我發誓你確實是個紳士！你的聲音、面容、四肢、動作和精神，皆說明你是出身自一流的血統。（她思考。）不能太快……慢點、慢點！倘若那人即是他家主人……怎麼辦？會有人這麼快就墜入愛河嗎？我想我感覺到這年輕人的完美，悄悄地入了我的眼簾。隨它去吧。（她高喊。）來人啊！馬伏里奧！（她從手指取下一枚戒指。）

（馬伏里奧再上。）

馬伏里奧：來了，小姐，聽候你的差遣。

奧麗維婭（將戒指交予他）：快去追上方才那個無禮的信差，公爵派來的人，他遺落了這枚戒指，也沒問我要不要它。告訴他我不會收下！請他莫要對他家主人拐彎抹角，抑或是給他虛假的盼望，我並不適合他。倘若那年輕人明日還會再來，我會將我的理由告知予他。快去吧，馬伏里奧！

馬伏里奧：小姐，我會的。

（馬伏里奧下。）

奧麗維婭：我已控制不了我的言行！恐怕我的眼睛可能蒙騙我。命運啊，展現你的力量，我們無法控制自己的宿命，該來的總是會來！

（奧麗維婭下。）

第二幕

●第一場 ——————————————————— P. 035

（海濱；安東尼奧與西巴斯辛上。）

安東尼奧：我不能與你同往嗎？

西巴斯辛：原諒我，不能，我近來厄運不斷。我的厄運可能
會影響你，就讓我獨自承受苦難吧。

安東尼奧：告訴我你欲往何處。

西巴斯辛：這不好說，先生，我計畫的行程是漫無目的地流
浪。我知道你知情達禮，不會堅持逼問我意欲保密之事，
但是我基於禮貌必須告訴你，我的本名乃是西巴斯辛，而
非先前所言之羅德里戈。家父是梅薩林的西巴斯辛，死後
留下我和我的孿生姊妹。我倆是同一時辰出生的；倘若天
意應允，我倆亦會同日死！但是你改變了命運，先生，在你
從海裡將我救起之前約莫一小時，我的姊妹已然溺斃。

安東尼奧：好可怕啊！

西巴斯辛：雖然她的相貌與我相似，但是許多人認為她貌若
天仙。在我眼裡的她是這樣的：她有一顆美麗的心。如今
她已溺斃於海中，先生，（他哽咽。）我似乎用淚水淹沒了對
她的記憶。

安東尼奧（發現西巴斯辛是一位紳士）：原諒我，先生，如此款
待不周。

西巴斯辛：喔，好安東尼奧，原諒我帶來這麼多麻煩。

安東尼奧：倘若你不願我為我的愛而死，那就讓我為你效勞
吧。

西巴斯辛：除非你想收回你潑出去的水——亦即殺死你方才
搭救之人——否則莫要如此要求。暫且告別了，我已對你

產生情誼，稍有觸及即可能使我落淚。我即將前往晉見奧西諾公爵，再會了。

（西巴斯辛下。）

安東尼奧：願眾神與你同往！奧西諾公爵的朝臣多與我為敵，否則我必隨你前去。（他轉身欲離去，又駐足考慮再三。）但是無論如何，我很享受你的友誼，那危險似乎也成了樂趣——我還是去吧！

（安東尼奧下。）

● 第二場 ────────────────── P. 038

（在街上；薇奧拉與馬伏里奧上。）

馬伏里奧：你方才莫不是和奧麗維婭女伯爵相談？（遞上一枚戒指。）她意欲將此戒指交還予你，先生，你將之取走即可省下我不少麻煩，請務必轉告公爵閣下她不願與他有任何瓜葛。還有一件事：你莫要再如此大膽，為了他的事前來叨擾——除非是回報他對此事的回應。（將戒指扔在地上。）收回去吧。

薇奧拉（駐足思考，然後想清楚情況）：我不想收回這枚戒指。

馬伏里奧：先生，你無禮地將之強交予她，她命我以同法交還予你。倘若它值得你屈身撿拾，那你便從地上撿起它；倘若不值，就任憑別人去撿吧。

（馬伏里奧下。）

薇奧拉：我並未給她任何戒指，她此乃何意？但願不是我的外表吸引了她！她如此仔細地打量我，似乎是看得瞠目結舌。她必定是愛上了我，透過這無禮的信差傳達了她的愛意。（**輕蔑地。**）她不願收下我家公爵的戒指！他並未送她戒指啊！倘若我真是她所愛之人，可憐的小姐，她的愛意恐將化為幻影。我的偽裝成了一種罪惡，對惡魔可謂是助紂為虐。相貌英俊卻虛假之人，竟如此輕易地贏得女人的芳心！哎呀，此乃起因於人性的弱點，而非人的本身；上天創造的我們本應如何，即是如何。（**她思忖。**）此事將會如何發展？我家主人如此深愛著她，而我這可憎之人卻同樣愛慕著他，殊不知她似乎愛上了我偽裝的他。結果將會如何？偽裝成男子，我毫無可能獲得我家主人的愛。喔，時間啊，是你必須解開此結，而不是我；此結難解，非我所能解之！

（**薇奧拉下。**）

●第三場

（在奧麗維婭家中的一個房間。托比・培爾契爵士與安德魯・艾古契克爵士上，兩人皆已酒醉。）

托比爵士：好了啦，安德魯爵士，時過午夜仍未就寢即是早起，你明知道。

安德魯爵士：不，我發誓我不知道，熬夜不睡即是熬夜不睡。

托比爵士：那是謬誤的邏輯，我憎恨它有如憎恨一杯未斟滿的酒！時過午夜而不睡，繼而再去就寢即是早寐，我們的生活不就是由火、水、空氣和土等四種元素所構成嗎？

安德魯爵士：話是這麼説的，但我認為生活乃是由吃吃喝喝所構成的。

托比爵士：你是博學多聞的學者！所以就讓我們吃吃喝喝吧。（叫喚：）我說瑪利婭！來點酒！

（費斯特上。）

費斯特：今天可好，我的朋友們？

托比爵士：歡迎你，傻子，現在唱首歌來聽聽吧。

安德魯爵士：真沒想到，傻子的嗓音可真好聽。（對費斯特：）你昨晚罕見地情況很好！餘興節目非常精采。這是打賞的錢，唱首歌來聽聽。

費斯特：你們想聽情歌，或是關於人生有多美好的歌曲？

托比爵士：情歌，就情歌吧。

費斯特（用魯特琴自彈自唱）：喔，我的情人，你在何處流浪？喔，駐足聆聽，你的真愛已然臨降，四下遊蕩為你歌

唱。美麗愛人，莫再離去，愛侶們重逢即結束旅行，所有智者之子皆心知肚明。

安德魯爵士：好極了，唱得好！

托比爵士：好，很好。

費斯特（唱歌）：愛是何物？並非從今往後，眼前的愉悅可使人歡笑快活，未來仍不知會發生什麼。光陰莫要躊躇虛擲，給我一吻吧，妙齡女子，青春一去不回頭！

安德魯爵士：悅耳的嗓音，一如我是真正的騎士。

托比爵士：不如我們來合唱一曲？

安德魯爵士：倘若你愛我，那就來吧。就唱「你這無賴」，你起個音，傻子，第一句是「緊閉你的嘴」。

費斯特：倘若我緊閉我的嘴，我就無法起音了。

安德魯爵士：很好！來吧，起個音。

（他們唱歌。瑪利婭上。）

瑪利婭：你們如此地吵鬧！倘若我家小姐不吩咐她的管家馬伏里奧將你們逐出去，那就再也莫要相信我了。

托比爵士：咱們家小姐生性拘謹，馬伏里奧像個老嫗似的，況且——（唱歌。）我們是三個快活的人兒！胡說八道，小姐。

費斯特：我發誓，這位騎士的情況很罕見。

安德魯爵士：是的，他只要心情好就會有不錯的表現，而我亦然。他的行事風格是比較好，但是我做起來較為自然。

托比爵士（唱歌）：喔，十二月的第十二天——

瑪利婭：看在上帝的分上，安靜！

（馬伏里奧上。）

馬伏里奧：諸位是瘋了不成？你們是神志紊亂或是不懂禮貌？竟如此喧嘩吵鬧，將我家小姐的府邸當成了酒館。難道你們不懂尊重？托比爵士，請容我直言，我家小姐歡迎你這親戚來訪，但是她不喜歡你的行為毫無分寸。倘若你能安守本分，那便留下；倘若不能——又倘若你願意離開——她非常樂意送你上路。

托比爵士：難道你不只是個管家嗎？只因你品德高尚，就要我們也如此？

費斯特：是的，我以聖安妮起誓！玩樂結束了！

托比爵士：果真如此？去吧，先生，將咱們小姐戴在你脖子上的頸圈擦亮吧。（*叫喊。*）再來點酒，瑪利婭！

馬伏里奧：瑪麗小姐，倘若你重視我家小姐的忠告，莫要再斟酒給這劣行之人。（*揮動他的拳頭。*）我要用這隻手向她稟報此事。

（*馬伏里奧下。*）

瑪利婭：去抖動你的耳朵吧，你這驢子！

安德魯爵士：這就如同決鬥時不到場，使人出洋相！

托比爵士：向馬伏里奧下戰書吧，騎士先生！我會親自將戰書交予他。

瑪利婭：親愛的托比爵士，今晚暫且有點耐心。自從公爵今日派那個年輕人前來拜訪我家小姐，她始終心神不寧。馬伏里奧就交給我吧！我能使他成為愚蠢的笑柄。

托比爵士：告訴我們該怎麼做！告訴我們該怎麼做！

瑪利婭：他自以為美德兼備，凡見著他之人皆會愛他。此一弱點將使他覆沒。

托比爵士：你意欲何為？

瑪利婭：我會在他必經之處落下幾封情書，信上會充滿愛意地描述他鬍子的顏色、他的腿形、他走路的姿態和他的眼神表情。我可以模仿我家小姐的字跡，有時候我們甚至分不清是何人所寫。

托比爵士：太好了！我嗅到了蹊蹺。

安德魯爵士：我也嗅到了。

托比爵士：他會以為那些情書是我姪女所寫，心想她必定是愛上了他。

瑪利婭：我敢打賭結果必是如此，我非常確定。

安德魯爵士：喔，是啊，真是太好了！

瑪利婭：這必然有趣至極，我向兩位保證；我知道此法必定對他有效。二位可隨同費比恩，藏匿在他將找到那封信之處，然後看著他如何解讀。但是今晚：去睡吧，再見了。

（瑪利婭下。）

安德魯爵士：相信我，她深諳此道！

托比爵士：而且她愛慕我，你作何看法？

安德魯爵士：我也曾被人愛慕過。

托比爵士：我去溫熱些許的雪莉酒，現在就寢也嫌太晚了。走吧，騎士！

（托比爵士與安德魯爵士下。）

（在公爵宮殿中的一個房間；公爵、薇奧拉、丘里奧與其他人上。）

公爵：早安！來點音樂吧。（對薇奧拉：）請吧，好西薩里奧，就唱昨晚那首古怪的老歌謠。來，唱個一小段即可。

丘里奧：倘若閣下願意，應該獻唱的是弄臣費斯特，他就在這府邸內的某處。

公爵：去尋他前來，並暫且彈奏樂曲吧。（丘里奧下。音樂演奏。）（對薇奧拉：）過來，孩子。倘若你有朝一日墜入愛河，在甜美的痛苦之中請你勿忘我：因所有真心相愛之人皆如我這般──情緒起伏，對每件事反覆無常，但是他們都著迷於被愛之人。你可喜歡這首曲子？

薇奧拉：完全呼應了愛情所在的寶座。

公爵：你此言有如專家一般！我敢打賭即便你年紀尚輕，應已有了心儀之人，可不是嗎，孩子？

薇奧拉：是有一點──倘若我能這麼說。

公爵：她是怎樣的女子？

薇奧拉：正如同閣下一般。

公爵：那她便配不上你了。她芳齡幾何？

薇奧拉：約莫與你相仿，閣下。

公爵：哎呀，年紀太大了！女子理應嫁給年齡較長之人，如此她才能調適自己以配合他，在她夫君心中也才能保有穩定的一席之地，因無論我們如何自滿，孩子，男人的感情是起伏不定的，充滿欲望和善變──較女人的心更容易迷失和受到誘惑。

薇奧拉：我想你說得對，閣下。

公爵：那就找個年紀比你輕的對象吧，否則你們的感情不會長久，因女人好似玫瑰，曾被展示的美麗花朵，未幾即會枯萎凋零。

薇奧拉：正是如此。哎呀，在臻至完美的當下即死去！

（丘里奧與費斯特再上。）

公爵：喔，好傢伙，來吧——唱你昨晚唱的那首歌曲。

費斯特：你可準備好了嗎，先生？

公爵：是的，請唱吧。

費斯特（隨著音樂演唱）：去吧、去吧，死亡，就讓我躺臥在悲傷的柏樹上。飛啊，飛啊，氣息，美麗而殘酷的女子殺我於無形。我的白色壽衣，全糾結在紫杉樹上。喔，作好準備！

公爵（給他錢）：這是獎賞你的辛勞。

費斯特：並不辛勞，先生，我因歌唱而歡愉。

公爵：那我就花錢買你的歡愉吧。

費斯特：是啊，先生，偶爾也該有人為歡愉付出代價。

公爵：至此即已足夠！

費斯特：願眾神庇佑你，再見了。

（費斯特下。）

公爵：你們其他人也退下吧。

（丘里奧與侍從們下。）

公爵（對薇奧拉）：再次前去拜訪那位殘酷的淑女吧，西薩里奧，讓她知道我高尚的愛毫不在意龐大的污穢地產，讓她知道吸引我的靈魂飄向她的是她的美貌；她貌美似天仙，是坐擁寶石的女王。

薇奧拉：但是倘若她無法愛你又該如何，閣下？

公爵：我不接受這個回答。

薇奧拉：是啊，但是你不得不接受。假設有某個女子——或許真可能如此——愛你至深，如同你愛奧麗維婭一般，而你卻無法愛她，也如實告知予她，難道她能不接受你這個回答？

公爵：未有女人的心可承受如愛情賦予我心這般強烈的熱情。未有女人的心足夠寬大可以容納！女人的心太善變了。哎呀，她們的愛只不過是口腹之欲，並非起源於情感，而是受味覺所驅使。但是我的口腹之欲有如海水一般飢渴，亦能消化大海一般的容量。莫要拿女人對我的愛與我對奧麗維婭的愛相比。

薇奧拉：是的，但是我知道——（她欲言又止，深恐暴露自己的身分。）

公爵：你知道何事？

薇奧拉：我知道女人能有多愛男人。事實上，她們有著如我們一般真誠的心。我父親有個女兒也曾愛上一名男子——如同我這般敬愛閣下——倘若我是個女子。

公爵：她有著怎樣的故事？

薇奧拉：一片空白，閣下，她未曾表露她的愛意，而是任由她的秘密，如花蕾中的蟲子似地啃食她玫瑰般的臉頰。她飽受相思之苦，因悲傷而憔悴。這難道不是愛？我們男人說的更多，立下的誓言也更多，但是我們的行為並不真摯。我們經常是信誓旦旦卻愛得少。

公爵：但你的姊妹是否因愛而死，我的孩子？

薇奧拉：我乃家父所有的女兒，亦是他所有的兒子——但或許是我想錯了。（她仍希望西巴斯辛並未溺死。）閣下，要我去拜訪那位小姐嗎？

公爵：是的，我正有此意。（交給薇奧拉一件珠寶。）速速去探訪她，將這件珠寶交予她，就說我的愛不容拒絕。

（公爵與薇奧拉下。）

（奧麗維婭的花園；托比・培爾契爵士、安德魯・艾古契克爵士與費
比恩上。）

托比爵士：來吧，費比恩先生。

費比恩：我來了。倘若這場好戲我錯過了一絲一毫，但願我被
　　悲慘地滾沸而死！

托比爵士：看這隻下流卑賤的狗蒙受如此之羞辱，你難道不
　　覺得欣喜？

費比恩：我會欣喜若狂！

（瑪利婭上。）

托比爵士：那個小惡徒來了！一切可好，我的寶貝？

瑪利婭：你們三個，全都躲到樹籬後面，馬伏里奧來了！他頂
　　著烈日練習對著自己的影子鞠躬作揖。為了嘲笑他，仔細
　　看好！這封信必能使他出糗。躲起來，以惡作劇之名！

（男人們躲起來，瑪利婭則扔下一封信，然後她下。馬伏里奧上。）

馬伏里奧：一切皆乃運氣使然。瑪利婭曾說奧麗維婭喜歡
　　我，我亦聽聞暗示，倘若她喜歡過任何人，那必是如我這
　　般的人。況且，她待我的尊重更勝於對其他人。對此我該
　　作何感想？

托比爵士：好個自負的惡棍啊！

費比恩：噓！思慮使他成了珍稀的孔雀，瞧他在開屏之後如何
　　昂首闊步！如今他深陷在思慮中，滿腦充斥著想像。

馬伏里奧：我可想見自己坐在我的王者寶座上──

托比爵士（憤怒地）：喔，我恨不得現在有塊石頭讓我扔向他
　　的眼睛！

馬伏里奧：——召喚我的僕人們前來服侍我，穿著我華麗的絲絨睡袍，從奧麗維婭仍在熟睡中的沙發床上起身——

托比爵士（更憤怒地）：我氣得火冒三丈！

費比恩：喔，安靜、安靜。

馬伏里奧：——我會派人去尋來我的叔父托比。

托比爵士（怒不可遏地）：是可忍，孰不可忍！

費比恩：喔，安靜、安靜！

馬伏里奧：我派了七名下人恭順地前去尋他，同時我蹙眉，或許調緊我的懷錶，抑或是把玩一枚貴重的珠寶。托比前來朝著我作揖。

托比爵士（至此已完全暴怒如雷）：還能讓這傢伙活著嗎？

費比恩：即便有野馬試圖從我們口中拖出隻字片語，還是務必保持緘默！

馬伏里奧：我如此般向他伸出我的手（他伸出一隻癱軟的手。），收回平常的笑臉，作出權威的表情——

托比爵士：托比沒當下賞你一巴掌嗎？

馬伏里奧：——我說：「托比叔父，既然我幸運娶得你的姪女，我有權這麼說。」

托比爵士：怎麼？怎麼說？

馬伏里奧：「你必須馬上戒酒。」

托比爵士：走開，你這卑鄙小人！

費比恩：耐心點，否則我們會壞了計畫。

馬伏里奧：「而且你還浪費寶貴的時間與一名愚蠢的騎士交好。」

安德魯爵士：他指的是我，告訴你！

馬伏里奧：「那個安德魯爵士。」

安德魯爵士：我就知道是我，許多人都說我愚蠢。

馬伏里奧（撿起那封信）：這是什麼？

費比恩：如今鳥兒已靠近陷阱了。

托比爵士：但願他會大聲唸出內容！

馬伏里奧：哎呀，這是我家小姐的字跡。（讀信。）「給我未知的仰慕之人：此信代表我的善意。」正是她的措辭。（他拆開封蠟。）信上還有她的私用封緘。是的，這確實是我家小姐的親筆信。這是要給誰的呢？

費比恩：此信必能完全地說服他。

馬伏里奧（讀信）：「天曉得我有心儀之人，但是誰呢？嘴唇，莫要動，不得讓任何人知情。」會不會是你呢，馬伏里奧？

托比爵士：絞死你，你這自吹自擂之人！

馬伏里奧：「沉默於我有如刀割，M、O、A、I主宰了我的人生。」

托比爵士：這女人可真有一套。

費比恩：她給他服下了致命的毒藥！

托比爵士：他竟然這麼快就中餌上鉤！

馬伏里奧：如今她用詩文寫著：「我能命令我心仰慕之對象。」哎呀，她能命令我啊！我服侍她——她是我家小姐。那些字母究竟是何意？M、O、A、I——那些字母在我的名字裡都有，但是順序並非如此。「倘若這封信落入你的手中，請仔細想想。因時運不同，我的身分高於你，但是莫要害怕地位之崇高！有些人天生地位崇高，有些人是憑實力而臻至偉大，有些人則是被強加以偉大。命運伸出了援手，讓你的勇氣和精神去擁抱命運，為你可能會有的未來作好準備，拋開你卑微的外表，煥然一新，公然對某位親戚表示敵意，對僕人們呼來喚去，讓你所言只談論高遠的志向，要富有創意；此乃為你嘆息的她給你的忠告。記住是誰曾恭維你的黃色長襪；我要你記住。去吧，幸運之神已然眷顧你，你只消接納；否則你亦可永世為管家，做僕人們的朋友，不值得碰觸幸運之神的手指。再見了。願意為你奴僕的她——幸運的不快樂之人。」此事已昭然若揭！我必然要驕傲，我將閱讀名人要士的著作，我將與托比爵士正面衝突，我將回避平庸的朋友們。一切皆在暗指：我家小姐愛我。她確實日前曾讚美我的黃色長襪；藉此（**他揮動這封信。**），她是在向我傾吐愛意，鼓勵我表現出她所喜愛的行徑。感謝命運使我如此幸運地墜入愛河，我將變得冷漠又驕傲，逮到機會便穿上黃色長襪。（**他將信紙反過來。**）背面還有附筆：「你必定知道我是何人。倘若你也愛我，請用微笑以示之；你的笑容如此地迷人。所以在我面前，請微笑，我親愛的甜心，我懇求你。」我會微笑；我會遵照她所有的要求。

（**馬伏里奧下。**）

155

費比恩：即使波斯國王給我一大筆錢，我也不願錯過這場惡作劇！

托比爵士：我可以為此騙局娶了那丫頭。

安德魯爵士：我也可以！

托比爵士：而且不向她要求任何嫁妝，只要再來個諸如此類的笑話即可。

（瑪利婭上。）

費比恩：我們的惡作劇大師來了！

托比爵士：待他的美夢幻滅之時，他必然會發瘋！

瑪利婭：説實話，你們覺得有用嗎？

托比爵士：無庸置疑！

瑪利婭：倘若你們想知道此惡作劇的發展，就看著他一見到我家小姐時的反應吧。他會穿著黃色長襪前來，她所憎惡的顏色；他會對著她微笑，恰巧與她此刻的心情相悖。你們也知道她生性悲觀，她必定會非常惱怒！倘若你們想親眼看到，就隨我來吧！

托比爵士：請帶路，你這惡作劇大師！

安德魯爵士：我也隨你們去。

（全體下。）

第三幕

● 第一場——————————————————————P. 063

（奧麗維婭的花園；薇奧拉上，費斯特帶著一只小鼓上。）

薇奧拉：歡迎你，朋友，以及你的音樂。你是依著擊鼓生活的嗎？

費斯特：不，先生，我是依著教堂生活的。

薇奧拉：你是神職人員嗎？

費斯特：不，先生，我是依著教堂生活，因我住在家中，而我的家就在教堂附近。

薇奧拉：所以你可以說國王是依著乞討生活的，倘若有乞丐生活在他的附近。或是說教堂和你的鼓相近，倘若那只鼓碰巧在教堂附近。

費斯特：你言之有理，先生！如此生逢其時！一個句子之於一個機智之人，有如一隻羔羊皮手套，可以輕易地由內而外被翻轉出來！

薇奧拉：看得出你天性快活，對凡事都無憂無慮。

費斯特：並非如此，先生，我是有憂慮的。只是我憑著良心發誓，先生，我並不擔心你。倘若此即對凡事都無憂無慮，先生，希望能使你化為隱形。

薇奧拉：你不是奧麗維婭小姐的傻子嗎？

費斯特：不，並不是，先生，奧麗維婭不喜好娛樂。她不願收留一個傻子，先生，除非她結了婚。傻子之於丈夫，如同沙丁魚之於鯡魚——丈夫是比較大的。我確實不是她的傻子，而是為她竄改文字之人。

薇奧拉：我日前才在奧西諾公爵府上見到你。

費斯特：我想我也在那兒見識到你的聰明。

薇奧拉：倘若你嘲笑我，我便不再多留片刻。且慢，（她翻開錢袋看。）這是給你的一點賞錢。（她給他一些錢。）你家小姐在嗎？

費斯特：小姐在屋裡，先生，我去讓她知道你來了。

（費斯特下。）

薇奧拉：他是個夠聰明的傻子，值得打賞。而且做得好就需要天資聰穎，他必須觀察打趣對象的情緒。如同一位智者的專業一般，這也是需要很努力的工作。要做得巧妙聰明，他才是個適切得體的傻子；但是當一位智者屈尊做傻事之時，他就會毀了自己的名聲。

（托比·培爾契爵士與安德魯·艾古契克爵士上。）

托比爵士：願上帝與你同在，紳士。

薇奧拉：你亦然，先生。

托比爵士：能否請你進屋裡？我姪女想請你進來，倘若你意欲與她相談。

薇奧拉：我確實想見見令姪女，先生。（奧麗維婭與瑪利婭從屋內走出來迎接她，薇奧拉開始唸她預先準備好的說詞。）最優秀又高雅的小姐，但願上天賜予你諸多恩典！我有個信息只能說給你一人聽。

奧麗維婭（對其他人）：關上花園的門，然後先回避吧。（托比爵士、安德魯爵士與瑪利婭下。）把你的手給我，先生。（她伸出她的手。）

薇奧拉（握著她的手鞠躬）：美麗的公主，我是你謙卑的僕人西薩里奧。

奧麗維婭：我的僕人，先生！你是奧西諾公爵的僕人。

薇奧拉：一如他是你的僕人，況且他的一切也將屬於你。你僕人的僕人也就是你的僕人，小姐。

奧麗維婭：對於他，我未曾想著他；對於他的心思，我但願他是滿腦空白，而非被我所充滿了！

薇奧拉：小姐，我是來此說服你對他的想法改觀。

奧麗維婭：喔，拜託你，我懇求你，莫要再提及他。但是倘若你堅持要說，在我聽來會比天堂的樂音更加悅耳。在你前次的迷人來訪之後，我差人送了一枚戒指給你。我那麼做是傷了我自己，也傷了我的僕人，恐怕亦傷害了——你。我以如此可鄙的方式硬將那枚戒指塞給了你，理應接受你的負面批評。你作何感想？

薇奧拉：我同情你。

奧麗維婭：那是朝向愛情前進了一步。

薇奧拉：不，就連一小步也沒有，眾所周知我們經常同情的是敵人。

奧麗維婭：那好吧，也該是我學習重拾笑容的時候了。（**時鐘敲響報時**。）時鐘提醒我在浪費時間。莫要擔心，好青年，我不會對你窮追不捨，但是待你成年之後，你的妻子會有個好夫君。（**她指向落日**。）那是你應走的路線：往西。

薇奧拉：那就往西吧！祝福小姐有幸福的人生。你沒有信息要捎給我家主人嗎？

奧麗維婭：稍待一會兒，能否請問你對我作何感想？

薇奧拉（**用謎語似地回答**）：一切皆不如表面上那般。（**她指的是：「你以為你愛的是個男人，但是其實不然。」**）

奧麗維婭（**以為薇奧拉是無禮相待**）：倘若我真的這麼想，我對你亦如是。（**她意思是：「我認為你很無禮。」**）

159

薇奧拉：那你想的就是對的，我並非如表面上那般。（她意思是：「我是個女人。」）

奧麗維婭：但願你是我希望的那般！（她意思是：「希望你能成為我的丈夫！」）

薇奧拉：那會比我現在這樣更好嗎？希望如此，因你使我顯得愚蠢。

奧麗維婭（自言自語）：喔，他生氣時的模樣可真是英俊！試圖掩藏的愛情，會比殺人罪行更快暴露出來。愛情如同白晝一般明顯可見。（大聲說。）西薩里奧，我以春天的玫瑰、處子之心、榮譽、事實和一

切起誓，我太愛你了無法掩藏。莫要對我的示愛話語作出任何錯誤的結論，你並未給我向你求愛的理由。就這麼想吧：有所回報的愛情固然好，但是未求回報的愛情更好。

薇奧拉：我發誓我的心、我的忠誠和我的真實皆屬於我，未有任何女人得之，將來也不會有，除了我之外。所以再見了，好小姐，我再也不會為我那以淚洗面的主人前來向你示愛了。

奧麗維婭：請你務必再來，或許你能感動我的心接受他的愛。（奧麗維婭與奧薇拉下。）

（在奧麗維婭家中的一個房間；托比·培爾契爵士、安德魯·艾古契
克爵士與費比恩上。）

安德魯爵士：不，我將不再久留。

托比爵士：但是為什麼呢，安德魯爵士？

安德魯爵士：我看到令姪女對那公爵的僕人，遠比她待我更好。我在花園裡親眼所見。

托比爵士：她在那兒可有見到你，老朋友？

安德魯爵士：如我現在看著你似地一清二楚。

費比恩：那她這麼做顯然是為了使你妒忌，你應該和那青年決鬥才是。如今你在她眼裡顯得軟弱，你必須儘快想想辦法。

托比爵士：挑戰公爵的僕人，與之決鬥，傷他十一處，我姪女必能聽聞此消息。聽聞你的英勇事蹟必將使她對你印象改觀。

費比恩：別無他法了，安德魯爵士。

安德魯爵士：二位誰能前去向他下戰帖？

托比爵士：去吧，以強而有力的字跡寫下戰書，要言簡意賅、切中要點。快去吧！

安德魯爵士：我上哪兒能找到你？

托比爵士：我們會在寫作室與你會合，去吧。

（安德魯爵士下。）

費比恩：他是你親愛的小傀儡，托比爵士。

托比爵士：他對我甚為珍視，小伙子——我花了他約莫兩千英鎊。

費比恩：他應該能寫出荒謬可笑的一封信。你會去遞送嗎？

托比爵士：倘若我不去，就莫要再信任我了。我也會竭力確保那位青年有所回覆，只是我認為即使用公牛和繩索也不可能拉近他們。

費比恩：他視之為對手的那位青年，臉上也看不出有殘酷的痕跡。

（瑪利婭上。）

托比爵士：你瞧，咱們的小鳥兒來了。

瑪利婭：倘若你們想捧腹大笑，隨我來吧。馬伏里奧那個白癡果真穿了黃色長襪！他謹遵我信上的每一點，笑到臉都僵硬了，保證你們沒看過那般的景象！我幾乎忍不住想朝著他扔東西了，相信我家小姐一定會打他；倘若她打了，他也會微笑著接受，當成莫大的恩賜。

托比爵士：走吧，帶我們去找他！

（全體下。）

●第三場———————————————P. 073

（街道上；安東尼奧與西巴斯辛上。）

西巴斯辛：我無意勞煩你，但是既然你喜歡如此費神，我便不再責罵你了。

安東尼奧：我無法坐視不管，我很擔心你的安危。未有嚮導或朋友隨行的陌生人，來到此地經常會遭遇危險。

西巴斯辛：我的好安東尼奧！我無言以對，只能感謝你。倘若
　　我的富有如同我對你的虧欠一般多，你應能得到豐厚的報
　　償。現在該怎麼做？要在這個城鎮觀光嗎？

安東尼奧：明日再去吧，先生，先為你找個落腳處。

西巴斯辛：我並不累，而且時候尚早。我們且去觀光吧。

安東尼奧：請你諒解我——我走在這街道上可能會有危險。
　　曾經在海上與公爵的船艦起衝突之時，我是始作俑者；其
　　嚴重程度，事實上，倘若我在此被人發現，恐怕是必死無
　　疑。

西巴斯辛：你殺了他的許多手下？

安東尼奧：那次衝突未有流血事件，只要將我們向他們強取
　　之物歸還即可解決爭端。事實上，就貿易行商而言，本市
　　多數居民皆已歸還所取之物，唯有我並未歸還，為此——
　　倘若我在此被人發現——我將要付出極大的代價。

西巴斯辛：那就別太招搖過市了。

安東尼奧：這是我的錢袋。最好還是下榻在南區市郊的大象
　　客棧吧，我來點餐，你先去四處觀光，稍後再去那兒與我
　　會合。

西巴斯辛：何以要我取走你的錢袋？

安東尼奧：你可能會看到一些你有意購買的紀念品，你應該
　　沒有多餘的錢能購置奢侈品吧，先生。

西巴斯辛：那我就拿著你的錢袋，暫且離開你一小時。

安東尼奧：前往大象客棧……

西巴斯辛：我會記住的。

（全體下。）

（奧麗維婭的花園；奧麗維婭與瑪利婭上。）

奧麗維婭（自言自語）：我差人前去尋他，他說他會來。我應
　　如何款待他？我該給他什麼？因青春易買，不易求得或商
　　借。我說得太大聲了。（對瑪利婭：）馬伏里奧何在？他正經
　　又拘禮──考量我目前的情況，此乃僕人的好特質。馬伏
　　里奧何在？

瑪利婭：他馬上就來，小姐：但是很奇怪，他似乎著了魔。

奧麗維婭：怎麼，發生何事？他在胡言亂語嗎？

瑪利婭：不，小姐，他就只是微笑。奉勸小姐提高警覺，我
　　相信此人已心神錯亂。

奧麗維婭：去找他來。（瑪利婭下。）我和他同樣發狂了──倘
　　若悲傷的發狂和快樂的發狂是同樣的。（馬伏里奧上。）你
　　好，馬伏里奧。

馬伏里奧（笑得開懷地）：親愛的小姐，你好。

奧麗維婭：你在微笑？我差人去找你來是因為我很悲傷。

馬伏里奧：悲傷，小姐？何以悲傷？你沒注意到我的黃色長
　　襪嗎？可想而知你應該覺得賞心悅目。

奧麗維婭：你是怎麼搞的？

馬伏里奧：我並未充滿晦暗的想法，雖然我的雙腿是黃色
　　的。那封信上的指示我使命必達；你我都認得出那美麗的
　　羅馬字體。

奧麗維婭：你的行徑怪異，馬伏里奧。

瑪利婭：你好嗎，馬伏里奧？

馬伏里奧：你是在和我說話嗎？夜鶯會回應烏鴉嗎？

瑪利婭：你何以用如此大膽到荒謬的模樣，出現在我家小姐
　　面前？

馬伏里奧（對奧麗維婭）：「莫要害怕地位之崇高」——喔，這句話寫得可真好。

奧麗維婭：你在胡說什麼，馬伏里奧？

馬伏里奧：「有些人天生地位崇高」——

奧麗維婭：什麼？

馬伏里奧：「有些人憑實力而臻至偉大」——

奧麗維婭：你究竟在說什麼？

馬伏里奧：「有些人則是被強加以偉大」——

奧麗維婭：但願上天能治癒你！這著實是仲夏的瘋病！

（一名僕人上。）

僕人：小姐，奧西諾公爵的年輕紳士已然返回。好不容易才說服他回來，他在等候小姐的差遣。

奧麗維婭：我這就去見他。（僕人下。）好瑪利婭，好好照顧這傢伙。（她指向馬伏里奧。）我的叔父托比何在？我得找幾個人特別照料他，即便傾盡我的半數財產也不能讓他吃苦頭。

（奧麗維婭與瑪利婭下。）

馬伏里奧：喔，哎呀！事情愈來愈明朗了，竟然委請托比爵士來照顧我！情況和那封信的內容一致。她在寫信之時，就蓄意請他來此，好讓我對他「公然表示敵意」。這一切皆合邏輯，未有絲毫的疑慮，毫無阻礙，誰也阻止不了我實現我的願望！此乃天意，非我之所為，要感謝上天啊！

（瑪利婭帶著托比·培爾契爵士與費比恩再上。）

托比爵士：以神聖的一切為名，他在何處？

費比恩：他在這兒，他在這兒。（對馬伏里奧：）你好嗎，先生？

馬伏里奧：走開，我厭惡你，讓我享有我的隱私權。你走吧！

瑪利婭：瞧瞧他的行徑如此怪異！他彷彿是被惡魔附身一般。我不是告訴你了嗎？托比爵士，我家小姐請你好好照顧他。

馬伏里奧：哈哈！果真如此？

托比爵士（對瑪利婭與費比恩）：且慢！我們必須溫和地待他，就交給我吧。（對馬伏里奧：）你好嗎，馬伏里奧？一切可都好？要違抗惡魔！記住，他是全人類的敵人。

馬伏里奧：你可知道你在說什麼？

瑪利婭（對托比爵士與費比恩）：要注意，倘若你們說了惡魔的壞話，他可是有仇必報的。祈禱上帝他不是著了魔。

托比爵士：請你安靜，你看不出他覺得惱怒了嗎？將他交給我吧。

費比恩：你必須溫和以待，要溫和！溫和！惡魔是暴烈的，不容別人粗魯以待！

托比爵士（對馬伏里奧）：你好，我的小鳥兒。你好嗎，小雞仔？

馬伏里奧：先生？

托比爵士：是的，小鴨仔，隨我來。怎麼！如你這般聰明之人，和撒旦玩遊戲可是不智之舉。絞死他，那個來自冥界的壞東西！

瑪利婭：帶他禱告吧，好托比先生。帶他禱告。

馬伏里奧：帶我禱告？

瑪利婭：不，我告訴你——他聽不得虔敬之事。

馬伏里奧：你們都去死吧，盡是遊手好閒的無用之人！我和你們不同，你們以後便會更瞭解我了。

（馬伏里奧下。）

托比爵士：這有可能嗎？

費比恩：倘若這是一部話劇，我會稱之為虛構的虛構故事！

托比爵士：他已落入這惡作劇的陷阱中——魚鉤、釣線和鉛錘！

瑪利婭：但是要趕緊跟上去，免得計畫被破壞了。

托比爵士：我有個主意：我們讓他穿著束衣關在一個漆黑的房間裡。我姪女已經相信他瘋了，我們可以繼續惡作劇，讓我們自己開心、也讓他痛苦，直到我們決定饒他一命。瞧瞧是誰來了！

（安德魯·艾古契克爵士上，拿著一張紙揮動著。）

費比恩：更多樂趣來了！

安德魯爵士：這是戰書，你看看，我向你保證內容文情並茂。

托比爵士：給我吧。（他讀信。）「青年，不論你是何人，總之你是個卑劣的傢伙。莫要懷疑我為何如此罵你，因我不會給你任何理由。」

費比恩：寫得不錯，如此便在法律的規範之內。

托比爵士：「你前來探訪奧麗維婭小姐，她在我面前待你和善。你滿口謊言，但這並非我要挑戰你的理由。我會在你回家的途中埋伏攻擊你；倘若你運氣好殺了我，那你便是個無賴和惡徒。」

費比恩：你仍然在守法的範圍之內，很好。

托比爵士：「再見了，但願上帝對你我當中的一人慈悲！祂可能會對我慈悲，所以你要小心。你的朋友，一如你待他，和你不共戴天的敵人安德魯·艾古契克。」倘若此信打動不了他，他的雙腿也動不了。我會將此信遞送給他。

瑪利婭：時機正好！他此刻正在和我家小姐相談，未幾便會離開。

托比爵士：去吧，安德魯爵士，在花園的角落裡等候他。你一見到他便拔劍，對他大肆咒罵。用威嚇人的自信大聲辱罵對方，可比實際的鬥劍更助長一個人的威名。快去吧！

安德魯爵士：咒罵的事就包在我身上！

（安德魯爵士下。）

托比爵士（對費比恩）：我不會將安德魯爵士的信交給那位年輕的紳士，他一看就會知道這是個笨蛋寫的，根本嚇唬不了他。反之，我會口頭轉述向他下戰帖，將艾古契克形容得英勇無比，使那位年輕的紳士懼怕他的憤怒、技藝和狂暴。兩人皆會害怕得光是眼神交換就能殺死對方。

（奧麗維婭與薇奧拉上。）

費比恩：他和令姪女一起過來了。躲起來，等他離開，然後再跟蹤他。

托比爵士：我暫且去想想要用什麼威嚇的言語挑釁他。

（托比爵士、費比恩與瑪利婭下。）

奧麗維婭：我對著鐵石心腸已說了太多，也太輕忽了自己的尊嚴。恐怕我是做錯了，但是強烈的感情驅使我不得不這麼做。

薇奧拉：我家主人的悲傷有如你的感情一般強烈。

奧麗維婭（對薇奧拉）：來，為我戴上這條項鍊，墜子裡有我的畫像。莫要推辭，它沒有舌頭可以惹惱你。我懇求你，明日再來訪。只要是符合名譽之事，你對我的要求我難道會推辭嗎？

薇奧拉：只有這個，你對我家主人的真愛。

奧麗維婭：我已將真心獻給你，又如何能再給他？

薇奧拉：我先告辭了。

奧麗維婭：明日再來吧，再見了。

（奧麗維婭下。托比‧培爾契爵士與費比恩再上。）

托比爵士：紳士，願上帝拯救你。

薇奧拉：你亦然，先生。

托比爵士：不論你有何武器，請準備好吧。我不知你如何錯
　　　待了他，但是你的挑戰者有如嗜血的獵犬。他在花園恭候
　　　你的大駕，快快拔劍準備應戰吧，因你的對手動作敏捷、
　　　技藝純熟又致命。

薇奧拉：你想必是誤解了，先生，我相信我未曾與人有過爭
　　　端。我記得一清二楚，從不曾與人結怨。

托比爵士：你會發現事實並非如此，我向你保證。倘若你珍
　　　惜你的性命，提高你的戒備吧，你的對手年輕力壯、技藝
　　　超群又憤怒激昂。

薇奧拉：請教你，先生，他是何人？

托比爵士：他是一位騎士，跪在地毯上被授與一把儀式劍，
　　　但他在私下鬥劍時可是有如惡魔一般。他殺過三個人，此
　　　刻他的憤怒唯有死亡和埋葬才能滿足他。「先發制人」是
　　　他的座右銘，你不接受就算了。

薇奧拉：我這就回屋裡請求小姐的保護。我並非鬥劍之人，
　　　聽聞有些人會蓄意挑起打鬥以示自身的勇氣；想必他正是
　　　此種人。

托比爵士：先生，不！他的憤怒源自於很正當的理由，所以你
　　　最好快去赴戰，遂了他的心願。你不得返回屋內，除非你
　　　與我兩劍相交。所以，去吧──否則你就舉劍向我。你必
　　　須決鬥──這是一定的──否則莫要再手持武器。

薇奧拉：如此既無禮又詭異！我懇求你，告訴我何以我會惹
　　　惱此位騎士。此事必定是因疏忽而起，而非我蓄意所為。

托比爵士：我會據實以告。費比恩先生，你留下來陪這位紳
　　　士，等我回來。

（托比爵士下。）

薇奧拉：請問先生，你可知道此事？

費比恩：我知道這位騎士對你甚是惱怒，他想與你決一死戰，其餘細節我便不得而知。

薇奧拉：我懇求你告訴我，他是怎樣的人？

費比恩：看著他的外表，你不會發現他打鬥時的驚人實力；他確為伊利里亞技藝最精湛、殘酷又致命的對手。你會對他讓步嗎？我可竭力為你與他議和。

薇奧拉：我將為此欠你極大的人情。

（*他們下；薇奧拉非常害怕；托比爵士與安德魯爵士再上。*）

托比爵士：哎呀，他有如惡魔一般可怕！我未曾見過如此劍術超群之士！他出劍之力道有如你腳踏地面，據說他曾是波斯國王的劍士。

安德魯爵士：真該死，我不願與他決鬥！

托比爵士：是，但他不肯冷靜下來，費比恩亦壓制不住他的怒氣。

安德魯爵士：可惡！早知道他如此勇敢又工於劍法，我說什麼也不會挑戰他。倘若他能就此罷休，我可以將我的愛駒灰卡皮雷贈予他。

托比爵士：我去探探他的說法。留在這兒，竭盡你的全力，此次必不需要戰個你死我活。（*自言自語。*）是啊，我要把你當馬兒一般操弄。

（*費比恩與薇奧拉再上。*）

托比爵士（*對費比恩*）：我讓他交出他的馬來解決爭端，我已說服他這青年有如惡魔似地駭人。

費比恩（*對托比爵士*）：他面色蒼白，彷彿被熊追捕似的！

托比爵士（對薇奧拉）：我已無力回天，先生，他誓言要與你一決生死，但是他對此一爭端重新考慮，此刻他認為已是不值一提。但他既已發誓便是一諾千金，仍然執意要與你決鬥；他保證不會傷你分毫。

薇奧拉（竊語）：祈願上帝保護我！我有意告訴他們我並非男子！

費比恩：倘若你見到他暴怒，就速速逃離。

托比爵士（對安德魯爵士）：去吧，安德魯爵士，事情已無可轉圜，那位紳士將與你決戰一回合以捍衛他的榮譽。依據決鬥的規則，他是無可避免了，但是他答應不會傷你分毫。去吧，快去啊！

安德魯爵士：祈禱上帝他能信守諾言！（他緊張地拔劍。）

薇奧拉：我向你保證此乃與我的意願相悖。（她緊張地拔劍，兩人皆閉上眼睛，手持著劍胡亂揮舞。安東尼奧上，見到他們顯然是要決鬥，他誤將薇奧拉認作西巴斯辛。）

安東尼奧（對安德魯爵士）：收起你的劍！倘若這位年輕紳士對你有所冒犯，且讓我來代他負責；倘若是你冒犯了他，我將代他向你挑戰。（安東尼奧熟練地拔出他的劍。）

托比爵士：你，先生！你是何人？

安東尼奧：為好友挺身而出之人！

托比爵士：倘若你代友出戰，則我亦準備迎戰！（托比爵士拔劍。）

費比恩：住手，托比爵士！住手！執法人員來了！

（兩名執法人員上。）

托比爵士（對安東尼奧）：我們稍後再繼續。

薇奧拉（對安德魯爵士）：先生，請你收起你的劍，我懇求你。

安德魯爵士（鬆了一口氣）：好的，先生，我會信守承諾。你定能輕鬆駕馭卡皮雷，牠甚為服從操縱。

執法人員一（指向安東尼奧）：就是此人，盡你的職責吧。

執法人員二：安東尼奧，我奉奧西諾公爵之命逮捕你。

安東尼奧：你認錯人了，先生！

執法人員一：不，先生，我沒認錯，我認得你，雖然你頭上並未戴著水手帽。將他帶走，他知道我熟識他。

安東尼奧：那我便悄然離去了。（對薇奧拉：）這一切皆是因尋找你所致，但事已至此、無可轉圜，我將俯首接受制裁。此刻我必須要回我的錢袋，你意欲何如？無法對你伸出援手的懊惱，更甚於我接受命運安排的無奈。你看似驚愕，但是望你能重拾笑顏。

執法人員二：隨我走吧，先生。

安東尼奧：我必須請你將那些錢還給我。

薇奧拉：什麼錢，先生？為償還你方才施與我的恩情，也有一部分是因為你陷入了困境，我暫且借你一些錢吧。我身上沒有太多錢；來，取走我一半的錢吧。

安東尼奧（憤怒地）：你現在要拒絕我嗎？難道我為你所做的一切皆不算數嗎？

薇奧拉：我不知你所言為何意，我在此之前未曾見過你。

安東尼奧：喔，我的老天！

執法人員二：走吧，先生，我們該走了。

安東尼奧：讓我再說幾句話。這位青年——我從死亡駭浪中救起了他，我出於神聖的情感幫助了他，我因他的形象高貴而為他全心奉獻。

執法人員一：這又與我們何干？我們這是在浪費時間，走吧。

安東尼奧：但是，喔，他竟是如此卑劣之人！西巴斯辛，你已使你美好的外表蒙羞。在這世上，未有比冷血心腸更大的缺失了，唯有薄情之人可被稱為醜陋。德行即是美，但是外表美麗之人，一旦內心邪惡，亦只是充滿惡毒的空盒子罷了。

執法人員一：這人瘋了！走吧，先生。

安東尼奧：帶路吧。

（執法人員們與安東尼奧下。）

薇奧拉（意會到安東尼奧所言為何意）：親愛的兄弟，是真的嗎？我是否被誤認作你了？他稱我為「西巴斯辛」，而我從鏡中得知我倆長得一模一樣；我是模仿他的外表作為我的偽裝。喔，倘若他真的還活在世上，那暴風雨就是仁慈而充滿愛的！

（薇奧拉下。）

托比爵士：這小子實在是太可恥了！他拒絕幫助他落難的朋友，他的怯懦問費比恩即可知。

費比恩：是的，他很怯懦，十足的懦夫。

安德魯爵士：天哪，那我再追上去毆打他！

托比爵士：去吧——痛打他一頓，但是莫要拔劍。

安德魯爵士：倘若我不——

（安德魯爵士下。）

費比恩：走吧，我們去看個究竟。

托比爵士：我敢打賭什麼事也不會發生。

（全體下。）

第四幕

● 第一場————————————————————————————————P. 095

（奧麗維婭府邸前面的街道；西巴斯辛與費斯特上。）

費斯特：你試圖假裝我並不是前來尋你？

西巴斯辛：走開，你這個痴傻的傢伙，莫要再來煩我！

費斯特：你裝得還真像啊。（諷刺地。）不，我不認識你，並非是我家小姐派我來尋你，因她有話想對你說，你的名字也並非西薩里奧；這甚至不是我自己的鼻子！原本既有的事實皆非如此！

西巴斯辛：請你去別處胡說八道吧，你並不認識我。

費斯特：我胡說八道！你在說什麼？我懇求你，莫要如此行徑怪異，告訴我該如何向我家小姐覆命。要我跟她說你這就來了嗎？

西巴斯辛：我懇求你，你這傻子，饒了我吧。這些錢給你；倘若你再久留，我定當好好教訓你！

費斯特：哎呀，你可真是慷慨。賞錢給傻子的智者必定會有好報——即便是十四年後。

（安德魯爵士、托比爵士與費比恩上。）

安德魯爵士（誤認為西巴斯辛就是薇奧拉）：現在，先生，我們又狹路相逢！這是給你的教訓！（他攻擊西巴斯辛。）

西巴斯辛（反擊）：這是我給你的回應！還有這個！還有這個！這裡的每個人都瘋了嗎？

托比爵士：住手，先生，否則我會將你的匕首拋過這屋子。

費斯特：我這就去通報我家小姐；即使你打賞我，我也不願與你易地而處。

（費斯特下。）

托比爵士（抓住西巴斯辛）：好了，先生，住手！

安德魯爵士：不，放開他，我要換個方法向他報仇；我要以毆打罪名將他告上法庭，倘若伊利里亞尚有律法存在。雖然是我先動手打他，但是這並無妨。

西巴斯辛（對托比爵士）：把你的手拿開！

托比爵士：好了，先生，我是不會放你走的。

（西巴斯辛掙脫開來。）

西巴斯辛：現在，你有何話可說？倘若你膽敢再前進一步，你就拔劍吧！

（西巴斯辛拔出他的劍。）

托比爵士：怎麼、怎麼？好吧，看來我得讓你這無禮之人淌點血了。

（托比爵士拔出他的劍。奧麗維婭上。）

奧麗維婭：住手，托比！

托比爵士：小姐？

奧麗維婭：非得每回皆如此嗎？你這可鄙之人，理應去山上或野蠻的洞穴，在那兒不需要知情識禮！遠離我的視線！（對西巴斯辛，誤將他認作薇奧拉。）親愛的西薩里奧，莫要惱怒。（對托比爵士：）你這畜生！滾離這裡！（托比爵士、安德魯爵士與費比恩下。）（對西巴斯辛：）高貴的朋友，這無禮的攻擊打擾了你的平靜，你且以智慧回應，而非憤怒。前來我府上，聽我告訴你這畜生惹了多少無意義的是非，然後你看待此事便可一笑置之了。他讓他的靈魂蒙羞！我牽掛你的半顆心被他嚇得半死。

西巴斯辛（全然困惑，不認得奧麗維婭）：這是怎麼回事？此乃何意？是我瘋了，還是我在作夢？（他看出奧麗維婭對他情深意重。）倘若這是在作夢，就讓我永遠沉睡吧。

奧麗維婭：請你隨我來，希望你能應允。

西巴斯辛：小姐，我願意。

奧麗維婭：喔，太好了！

（全體下。）

●第二場 ——————————————————— P. 099

（在奧麗維婭府上的一個房間；瑪利婭與費斯特上。）

瑪利婭：好了，穿上這件長袍和戴上這個鬍子，讓他相信你是
　　教區牧師托帕斯爵士。動作快，我去將托比爵士找來。

（瑪利婭下。）

費斯特：我來穿上這個偽裝自己；希望我是穿這般長袍行騙
　　術的第一人！

（托比・培爾契爵士與瑪利婭上。）

托比爵士：願上帝保佑你，牧師先生。

費斯特：祝你日安，托比爵士。

托比爵士（指向一扇門，門上有對話用的小格柵）：去看顧他，托
　　帕斯爵士。

費斯特（用假裝的聲音）：我說，你好啊！願上帝為這監獄帶來
　　和平！

馬伏里奧（從一間內室虛弱地說）：是誰在叫喊？

費斯特：教區牧師托帕斯爵士，前來探訪發狂的馬伏里奧。

馬伏里奧：托帕斯爵士、托帕斯爵士，好托帕斯爵士——去找我家小姐。

費斯特：你除了小姐們之外，不談論其他的事嗎？

托比爵士：說得好，牧師先生。

馬伏里奧：托帕斯爵士，從未曾有人如此被誤解。請你莫要認定我瘋了，只是他們將我囚禁於如此漆黑之處。

費斯特：你說此地是漆黑的？

馬伏里奧：伸手不見五指啊，托帕斯爵士！

費斯特：哎呀，這裡有凸窗和百葉窗可供採光，高處還有面向南、北二方的窗戶，如同黑檀木一般明亮，而你卻說此處伸手不見五指？

馬伏里奧：我並未發瘋，托帕斯爵士，此處確實是漆黑一片。

費斯特：瘋子，你錯了。我說這裡沒有漆黑，只有無知，而你被困於此處。

馬伏里奧：我說這屋裡漆黑如無知一般，我說未曾有人遭受如此之污蔑；我並未比你更瘋癲！問我幾個追根究柢的問題。

費斯特：畢達哥拉斯對野鳥的看法為何？

馬伏里奧：祖母的靈魂可能會附在鳥兒身上。

費斯特：你對此有何看法？

馬伏里奧：我認為靈魂是高尚的；我並不認同畢達哥拉斯的看法。

費斯特：再見了，繼續留在黑暗中。你必須認同畢達哥拉斯的看法，我才能宣稱你是神志清醒的；你必須害怕殺死鳥兒，深恐你祖母的靈魂被迫離開。再見了。

馬伏里奧：托帕斯爵士！托帕斯爵士！

托比爵士：我親愛的托帕斯爵士！

費斯特（對托比爵士）：我是個好演員！

瑪利婭：你即使不偽裝也能達成此一任務，他根本看不見你。

托比爵士：用你自己的聲音和他說話，然後再來告訴我他的情況如何。（對瑪利婭：）但願我們能免除此一惡作劇；倘若他能輕易地獲釋，希望能放他一馬，我姪女已對我深感嫌惡！不，我無法再繼續開這個玩笑。請你稍後前來我的房間。

（托比爵士與瑪利婭下。）

費斯特（用他自己的聲音在馬伏里奧的門外唱歌）：嗨，羅賓，快活的羅賓，告訴我你家小姐好不好。

馬伏里奧：傻子——

費斯特：我家小姐愛上另一個——是何人在叫我？

馬伏里奧：好傻子，幫我一個忙。給我一根蠟燭、一支筆、墨水和紙，因我是個紳士，我會在有生之年對你表達謝意。

費斯特：馬伏里奧先生！

馬伏里奧：是的，好傻子。

費斯特：哎呀，先生，你何以陷入瘋狂狀態？

馬伏里奧：傻子，從未曾有人如我這般遭人污衊；我與你一般神志清醒啊。

費斯特：如我一般神志清醒？那你果真瘋了，倘若你的神志不比傻子更清醒。

馬伏里奧：他們將我囚禁於此，使我待在黑暗中，差遣教區牧師來看顧我；他們是在不擇手段意欲將我逼瘋。

費斯特：請你務必謹言慎行，教區牧師在此。（用他偽裝成托帕斯爵士的聲音。）馬伏里奧，但願上帝能使你恢復神智！睡一會兒吧，莫要再含糊不清地胡言亂語。

馬伏里奧：托帕斯爵士——

費斯特（仍佯裝成托帕斯爵士）：莫要與他交談，好傢伙。（用他自己的聲音。）誰，我嗎，先生？不是我，先生。願上帝與你同在，好托帕斯爵士。（再佯裝成托帕斯爵士。）是的，阿們。（用他自己的聲音。）我會的，先生，我會的。

馬伏里奧：傻子、傻子、傻子，我說——

費斯特：先生，要有耐心。你意欲何如？我與你交談已是惹禍上身。

馬伏里奧：好傻子，幫我弄點光線和一些紙，我向你保證我和伊利里亞的任何人一樣神志清醒。

費斯特：但願如此，先生！

馬伏里奧：我以這隻手發誓，我是的。給我一些墨水、紙張和光線，將我寫下的信交給我家小姐，你將能得到比遞送其他任何信件更多的好處。

費斯特：我會幫你，但是請告訴我實話，你是真的瘋了，抑或是假裝如此？

馬伏里奧：相信我，我並未發瘋；我此言為真。

費斯特：不，我決不相信瘋子所言，直到我看見他的智力。我會給你弄點光線和紙筆墨水。

馬伏里奧：我會重重獎賞你，請你快去吧。

費斯特（唱歌）：我先走了，先生。但是我未幾即會再回來，先生。

（費斯特下。）

● 第三場 ──────────────────────── P. 105

（奧麗維婭的花園；西巴斯辛上，他仍不敢相信自己不是在作夢。）

西巴斯辛：這是空氣；那是燦爛的太陽；這是她送給我的珍珠，我能摸得到、也看得見。雖然我心中充滿驚異，但是這絕非瘋狂。所以安東尼奧何在？我在大象客棧尋他不著，但是他曾來過此地；聽說他在鎮上四處找尋我。此刻他的忠告可能價值萬金！這意外接踵而來的好運，實在令人費解。當我心試圖說明我並未發瘋之時，我試圖與之爭辯。抑或發瘋的是那位小姐，但倘若真是如此，她就不可能如此流暢又自信地操持她的家和管理她的僕人們；我無法理解。那位小姐來了！

（奧麗維婭與一位牧師上。）

奧麗維婭：莫要責怪我如此匆忙。倘若你存有善意，請與我和牧師前往附近的禮拜堂，在他面前和神聖的穹頂之下，向我立下婚姻中的愛情誓約，然後我的嫉妒和疑慮皆可平息。他會保密，直到你願意公開為止，屆時我們再舉行符合我身分地位的慶祝儀式。你意下如何？

西巴斯辛：我會順從此人，隨你同行；我既已立下誓言，必定永世信守為真。

奧麗維婭：那就請你領路吧，好牧師。但願耀眼的陽光能祝福我們結為連理！

（奧麗維婭、西巴斯辛與牧師下。）

第五幕

●第一場

（奧麗維婭府邸前面的街道；費斯特與費比恩上。）

費比恩：請你讓我看看他的信。

費斯特：請你莫再要求看信。

費比恩：這就有如送一條狗給某人之後再要回去。

（公爵、薇奧拉與侍從們上。）

公爵：你們可是奧麗維婭小姐的侍從，朋友們？請讓你們家小姐知道我來了。

費斯特：樂意之至，先生。

（費斯特下；安東尼奧與執法人員們上。）

薇奧拉：解救我的人來了。

公爵：那張臉我記得一清二楚，即使我上次見到它時，它在戰火煙硝中被抹黑了。他是一艘不值錢小船的船長，在對抗我軍艦隊最好的船艦時英勇無比，即使蒙受重大損失之人亦盛讚他的名聲與榮譽。（對執法人員們：）他所犯何事？

執法人員一：奧西諾，此人名為安東尼奧，他從克里特島搶走了鳳凰號及其上之貨物，後來又在你的小姪子提特斯失去他的腿時登上了老虎號。他涉及了一場私人爭鬥，我們在街頭逮捕了他。

薇奧拉：他幫了我的忙，先生，拔劍捍衛我的人身安全，後來他說了一些胡話，所以我認為他是瘋了。

公爵：知名的海盜！海上的盜賊！你何以愚蠢得來到此地自投羅網，任由你的敵人擺布？

安東尼奧：奧西諾，高尚的先生，請容我撇清你對我的指控。安東尼奧從不曾是盜賊或海盜——只是我與你為敵是有原因的。我是被巫術吸引來此；我解救了那個最忘恩負義之人，亦即在你身邊的那名男子。我從驚濤駭浪之中救起了他，當時他已是奄奄一息。我賦予他生命，再添上了我的愛。為了他，我來到此鎮上使自己曝於危險之中，在爭鬥中我拔劍捍衛他。當我被逮捕之時，他虛偽狡詐地當著我的面否認我倆的友誼。在一眨眼的轉瞬之間，他變得彷彿二十年未曾見到我一般，拒絕將我的錢袋交還予我，那可是我不到半小時之前才給他的啊。

薇奧拉（震驚地）：這怎麼可能？

公爵（對執法人員們）：他是幾時來到此地？

安東尼奧（親自回答）：是今天，閣下。在此之前的三個月，我們朝夕相處，未曾有片刻分離。

（奧麗維婭與侍從們上。）

公爵：女伯爵來了，好似天仙走在人間！（對安東尼奧：）至於你，你滿口瘋言瘋語；此一青年這三個月皆在我身邊為僕。但是，此事容後再議。（對執法人員們：）將他帶到一旁。

奧麗維婭：閣下有何貴事——除了他不能擁有之事以外——是奧麗維婭能效一己之力的？（她見到薇奧拉，誤將她認作她的新婚丈夫。）西薩里奧，你並未信守承諾。

薇奧拉（一頭霧水）：小姐？

公爵：高雅的奧麗維婭——

奧麗維婭：你有何話要說，西薩里奧？（看到公爵意欲開口說話，她阻止了他。）請稍候，閣下——

薇奧拉：閣下有話要說，我職責所在必須保持緘默。

奧麗維婭：倘若你還是要老調重彈，閣下，在我聽來似是惱人的號叫。

公爵：還是這般殘酷？

奧麗維婭：還是這般堅持不懈，閣下。

公爵：無謂的堅持！你這無禮的小姐，枉費我的靈魂在你這忘恩負義的神壇獻上了最虔敬的禱告！我該如何是好？

奧麗維婭：隨你高興便是了，閣下。

公爵：你聽聽看，自從你拒絕了我的愛，也因為我想我知道是何人取代我得到你的歡心，你始終是如此這般的冷血暴君！但是你心愛之人，我知道你深愛著他──他取代我坐上了你心中的那個寶座，我對天發誓我會將他從你那冷酷的眼裡拔除。（對薇奧拉：）隨我來，孩子，我的思緒充滿惡念。我要犧牲我摯愛的羔羊（他指的是薇奧拉。），藉此為難住在白鴿（他指的是奧麗維婭。）身體裡的烏鴉之心。

薇奧拉：我會欣然地同意死一千次，只要能給你心靈的平靜。

（公爵與薇奧拉準備離開。）

奧麗維婭：西薩里奧要去何處？

薇奧拉：隨我愛的男人而去──我愛他更甚於愛我自己的眼睛、更甚於愛我的生命、更甚於我對妻子的愛。倘若我有半句虛言，天上的眾神大可因我玷辱我的愛而懲罰我！

奧麗維婭（以為她要被拋棄了）：哎呀，我竟如此被人誤導！

薇奧拉：是何人誤導了你？何人膽敢如此苛待你？

奧麗維婭：難道你忘了嗎？已經過了這麼久嗎？去找那位牧師前來一問。

（一名侍從下。）

公爵（對薇奧拉）：走吧！

奧麗維婭：去哪兒，閣下？西薩里奧，我的夫君，留下吧。

公爵：夫君？

奧麗維婭：是的，夫君，他還能否認嗎？

公爵（對薇奧拉）：她的夫君，先生？

薇奧拉：不，閣下，我不是！

奧麗維婭：哎呀，否認自己的身分乃是懦弱之舉。莫要害怕，西薩里奧，接受你的好運吧，明知你是誰就要誠實面對！如此你便能和你懼怕之人同等偉大。（牧師上。）歡迎你，牧師！牧師，你知道我和這位年輕人之間發生的事，我懇請你如實道來。

牧師：這只合約永恆地結合愛情，兩人牽手確認，再由神聖的一吻予以印證，交換你們的戒指之後強化了這段關係；這個協約的完整儀式，由我這個神職人員封緘和見證。這是兩小時前才剛發生的事。

公爵（對薇奧拉）：喔，你這滿口謊言的兔崽子！待你滿頭白髮時會是何種模樣？抑或是你的狡詐會迅速成長到讓你自食惡果？那就再會吧，但願我們未來的路途不會再有交集。

薇奧拉：閣下，我發誓——

奧麗維婭：喔，莫要發誓！儘管你害怕，還是務必保有你的一點尊嚴。

（安德魯‧艾古契克爵士上，他的頭受了傷。）

安德魯爵士：我的老天啊，快找醫生！馬上找個醫生去救治托比爵士。

奧麗維婭：怎麼回事？

安德魯爵士：他劈砍了我的腦袋，也割傷了托比爵士的頭。救救我們！我願付出一百元的代價，只想回家。

奧麗維婭：這是誰幹的，安德魯爵士？

安德魯爵士：公爵的手下，那個叫西薩里奧的傢伙。我們以為他是個懦夫，孰料他竟是撒旦的化身！

公爵：我的手下西薩里奧？

安德魯爵士（剛注意到薇奧拉）：天哪，他在這兒！（對薇奧拉：）你莫名其妙就打破了我的頭！我所做之事乃是被托比爵士所逼迫。

薇奧拉：何以對我說話？我未曾傷害你。你莫名其妙就拔劍向我，但是我對你謹守禮節，並未傷害你。

安德魯爵士：倘若頭上流血算是受傷，那你便傷害過我！我猜想你是不將頭上流血當一回事！（托比・培爾契爵士上，喝醉了由費斯特領上來。）托比爵士來了，腿還跛著；他有話要說。倘若他並未喝醉，他必能給你更像樣的教訓！

公爵：好了，紳士！你可安好？

費斯特：喔，他一小時之前便喝醉了。今天上午八點鐘，他的眼睛便是呆滯無神。

托比爵士（結巴地）：那麼他便是個惡棍和結巴的傻子！我憎惡喝醉酒的惡棍！

奧麗維婭：將他帶走。是誰如此對待他們？

安德魯爵士：我來扶你，托比爵士，因我倆的傷口可以一同包紮。

奧麗維婭：扶他上床吧，為他治療傷口。

（費斯特、托比爵士與安德魯爵士下。西巴斯辛上。）

西巴斯辛：抱歉，小姐，是我傷了他。但即便他是我的親生兄弟，我亦會如此防衛自己。你看著我的眼神頗為奇怪，我看得出來是我冒犯了你。原諒我，親愛的小姐，看在我們日前才彼此立下誓約的分上。

公爵（非常震驚）：同一張臉孔、同樣的聲音、同樣的服裝樣式，卻是兩個人！

西巴斯辛（見到他的老友）：安東尼奧！喔，我親愛的安東尼奧！失去你之後的時光甚是難熬啊！

安東尼奧：你是——西巴斯辛？

西巴斯辛：莫非你還懷疑，安東尼奧？

安東尼奧：你是如何將自己一分為二？將一個蘋果切成兩半，亦不似此二人的相貌這般相像。何者為西巴斯辛？

奧麗維婭：不可思議！

西巴斯辛（看著薇奧拉）：那兒站的是我嗎？我未曾有過兄弟……我亦未有分身在此地和各處的特異能力。我是有個姊妹，被無情的海浪剝奪了性命。（對薇奧拉：）你與我是何關係？你的家鄉在何方？請問你尊姓大名？你的父母是何人？

薇奧拉：我來自梅薩林，我父親名為西巴斯辛，我的兄弟亦喚此名；他溺斃時的穿著和你相同。倘若靈魂能同時附在身體和服裝上頭，那你便是來嚇唬我們的。

西巴斯辛：我確實是個靈魂——但是我屬於我所誕生的實質世界。倘若你是個女人，既然其他的條件完全吻合，我見到你理應淚流滿面地説：「歡迎、歡迎，已溺斃的薇奧拉！」

薇奧拉：我父親的眉毛上有顆痣。

西巴斯辛：我父親亦然。

薇奧拉：他在我十三歲生日那天過世。

西巴斯辛：在我的靈魂中還記憶猶新。在我和我的孿生姊妹年滿十三歲那天，他的陽壽告終。

薇奧拉：倘若我們的幸福無法被阻止，除了我身上的這套男裝，那就讓我證明我是薇奧拉吧。隨我去見這鎮上的一位船長，我原本身穿的衣服目前在他家中。幸虧有他伸出援手，我才得以獲救，前來服侍這位貴族公爵；爾後我的全部人生，便完全獻給了這位小姐和這位閣下。

公爵：莫要感到驚駭——他有著貴族血脈。倘若此事為真，目前確實看似如此，則這場最幸運的船難我亦參與其中。

（對薇奧拉：）孩子，你曾對我說過上千次，你永遠不可能愛一個女人如你愛我這般。

薇奧拉：那些話我願意再發誓一遍！

公爵：將你的手給我，讓我看看你身著女裝的模樣。

薇奧拉：最初領我上岸的那位船長，正替我保管我的服裝。為了馬伏里奧所起了頭的法律案件，他日前已遭到逮捕。

奧麗維婭：他會釋放他的。去帶馬伏里奧來此，但是哎呀——我這才記起來，聽聞他已心神錯亂，可憐的紳士。

（費斯特再上，帶著一封信，費比恩尾隨在後。）（對費斯特：）他可安好，朋友？

費斯特：說實話，小姐，以他目前的處境，他算是安好無恙了。他寫了一封信要給你。

奧麗維婭：拆信讀出內容吧。

費斯特（用一種奇怪的聲音）：「我對天發誓，小姐——」

奧麗維婭：怎麼，你也瘋了嗎？

費斯特：不，小姐，我只是在讀瘋言瘋語。倘若小姐要我用恰當的方式讀信，請容許我用特別的聲音。

奧麗維婭：請吧，儘管你神志清醒，還是請你讀信。

費斯特：是，小姐。（讀信。）「我對天發誓，小姐，是你構陷了我，此事應該公諸於世。雖然你將我送進一個黑暗的房間，將我交予你那酒鬼親戚處置，但是我仍如小姐你一般神志清醒。我有你的親筆信，說服我用此般的言行舉止；這將為我辯護，亦將使你蒙羞。你要對我作何感想都隨你，我理應更加守禮，但是我此言乃出於不公平的待遇。
——被人利用而發狂的馬伏里奧。」

奧麗維婭：這是他親筆所寫？

費斯特：是，小姐。

公爵：這聽起來不像是發瘋了。

奧麗維婭：放他自由吧，費比恩，將他帶來此處。（費比恩下。）閣下，希望你能接受我為你的姻親，而非妻子。倘若你能同意，儀式將在同日舉行，就在我的府上，所有費用由我負責。

公爵：小姐，我欣然接受你的提議。（對薇奧拉：）你的主人免除了你的職務；至於你對他的服侍——如此不適合女人，目前為止亦是有辱你的高貴血統——既然你長久以來稱我為「主人」，我這就伸出我的手。（薇奧拉握住他的手。）從此之後，你將成為你主人的妻子。

奧麗維婭（對薇奧拉）：姊妹——這才是你真正的身分！

（費比恩再上，帶著馬伏里奧。）

公爵：此人即是那個瘋子？

奧麗維婭：是，閣下。你可安好，馬伏里奧？

馬伏里奧：小姐，你構陷了我，大大地構陷了我。

奧麗維婭：是嗎，馬伏里奧？事實絕非如此。

馬伏里奧：小姐，確實如此，請你親讀此信。（他將瑪利婭偽造的信交給她。）你不可否認這是你的封緘。那你就承認吧，老實告訴我，你何以要我帶著笑容和穿著黃色長襪前來？你何以要我對著托比爵士和僕人們蹙眉？又何以在我一切都照做之後，你又將我囚禁於黑暗的屋內，讓牧師來探望我，令我出醜、落人笑柄？告訴我為什麼。

奧麗維婭：哎呀，馬伏里奧，這並非是我的字跡，只是我承認字跡非常相似。無庸置疑，這是瑪利婭的字跡。我此刻回想起來，最初確實是瑪利婭將你發瘋之事告知予我，然後你帶著笑容前來，言行舉止如同此信的內容一般。這是有人巧妙地開了你一個玩笑；待我們查出是何人所為，再由你親自審判和決斷此案。

費比恩：親愛的小姐，請容我說句話。莫使任何口舌之爭或未來的爭端，破壞了此刻令我驚異的喜悅。祈望事情不會演變至此，我必須坦承是我和托比開了馬伏里奧這個玩笑，因我們不喜歡他高傲無禮的態度。瑪利婭是聽從托比爵士的命令寫下此信，他已迎娶她作為交換條件。這場玩笑如何成為傷人的惡作劇，過程可能使人捧腹大笑，而非意欲報復，尤其在公正地衡量雙方的怨憤不滿之後。

奧麗維婭（對馬伏里奧）：哎呀，你這可憐的傢伙！他們竟如此戲弄你！

馬伏里奧：我必將報復你們所有的人！

（馬伏里奧下。）

奧麗維婭：他果真受到嚴重的構陷。

公爵（對費比恩）：快去追上他！與他和解吧，他尚未將船長之事告知予我們。在此事辦妥之後，等待適當的時機，我們將一同舉辦神聖的婚禮。（對奧麗維婭：）親愛的姊妹，我們暫且留在此地。（對薇奧拉：）西薩里奧——你仍然身著男裝，我暫且如此稱呼你——來吧。（他把手臂伸出讓她挽著。）待你換穿其他的服裝之後，你將成為奧西諾的妻子和他心中的皇后。

（全體下。）

Literary Glossary • 文學詞彙表

aside 竊語

一種台詞。演員在台上講此台詞時,其他角色是聽不見的。角色通常藉由竊語來向觀眾抒發內心感受。

■ Although she appeared to be calm, the heroine's **aside** revealed her inner terror.

雖然女主角看似冷靜,但她的**竊語**透露出她內在的恐懼。

---

backstage 後台

一個戲院空間。演員都在此處準備上台,舞台布景也存放此處。

■ Before entering, the villain impatiently waited **backstage**.

在上台前,壞人在**後台**焦躁地等待。

---

cast 演員;卡司陣容

戲劇的全體演出人員。

■ The entire **cast** must attend tonight's dress rehearsal.

全體演員必須參加今晚的正式排練。

---

character 角色

故事或戲劇中虛構的人物。

■ Mighty Mouse is one of my favorite cartoon **characters**.

太空飛鼠是我最愛的卡通**人物**之一。

---

climax 劇情高峰

戲劇或小說中主要衝突的結局。

■ The outlaw's capture made an exciting **climax** to the story.

逃犯落網成為故事中最刺激的**精彩情節**。

---

comedy 喜劇

有趣好笑的戲劇、電影和電視劇，並有快樂完美的結局。

- My friends and I always enjoy a Jim Carrey **comedy**.
  我朋友和我總是很喜歡金凱瑞演的**喜劇**。

---

conflict 戲劇衝突

故事主要的角色較量、勢力對抗或想法衝突。

- *Dr. Jekyll and Mr. Hyde* illustrates the **conflict** between good and evil.
  《變身怪醫》描述善惡之間的**衝突**。

---

conclusion 尾聲；結局

解決情節衝突的方法，使故事結束。

- That play's **conclusion** was very satisfying. Every conflict was resolved. 該劇的**結局**十分令人滿意，所有的衝突都被圓滿解決。

---

dialogue 對白

小說或戲劇角色所說的話語。

- Amusing **dialogue** is an important element of most comedies.
  有趣的**對白**是大多喜劇中重要的元素之一。

---

drama 戲劇

故事，通常非喜劇類型，特別是寫來讓演員在戲劇或電影中演出。

- The TV **drama** about spies was very suspenseful.
  那齣關於間諜的電視**劇**非常懸疑。

---

event 事件

發生的事情；特別的事。

- The most exciting **event** in the story was the surprise ending.
  故事中最精彩的**事件**是意外的結局。

---

introduction 簡介

一篇簡短的文章,呈現並解釋小說或戲劇的劇情。

- The **introduction** to *Frankenstein* is in the form of a letter.
  《科學怪人》的**簡介**是以信件的形式呈現。

---

motive 動機

一股內在或外在的力量,迫使角色做出某些事情。

- What was that character's **motive** for telling a lie?
  那個角色說謊的**動機**為何?

---

passage 段落

書寫作品的部分內容,範圍短至一行,長至幾段。

- His favorite **passage** from the book described the author's childhood.
  他在書中最喜歡的**段落**描述了該作者的童年。

---

playwright 劇作家

戲劇的作者。

- William Shakespeare is the world's most famous **playwright**.
  威廉莎士比亞是世界上最知名的**劇作家**。

---

plot 情節

故事或戲劇中一連串的因果事件,導致最終結局。

- The **plot** of that mystery story is filled with action.
  該推理故事的**情節**充滿打鬥。

---

point of view 觀點

由角色的心理層面來看待故事發展的狀況。

- The father's **point of view** about elopement was quite different from the daughter's. 父親對於私奔的**看法**與女兒迥然不同。

---

prologue 序幕

在戲劇第一幕開始前的介紹。

■ The playwright described the main characters in the **prologue** to the play.
劇作家在**序幕**中描述了主要角色。

....

quotation 名句

被引述的文句；某角色所說的詞語；在引號內的文字。

■ A popular **quotation** from *Julius Caesar* begins, "Friends, Romans, countrymen . . ."
《凱撒大帝》中常被**引用的文句**開頭是：「各位朋友，各位羅馬人，各位同胞……」。

....

role 角色

演員在劇中揣摩表演的人物。

■ Who would you like to see play the **role** of Romeo?
你想看誰飾演羅密歐這個**角色**呢？

....

sequence 順序

故事或事件發生的時序。

■ Sometimes actors rehearse their scenes out of **sequence**.
演員有時會不按**順序**排練他們出場的戲。

....

setting 情節背景

故事發生的地點與時間。

■ This play's **setting** is New York in the 1940s.
戲劇的**背景設定**於 1940 年代的紐約。

....

soliloquy 獨白

角色向觀眾發表想法的一番言論，猶如自言自語。

■ One famous **soliloquy** is Hamlet's speech that begins, "To be, or not to be . . ."

哈姆雷特最知名的**獨白**是：「生，抑或是死……」。

....

symbol 象徵

用以代表其他事物的人或物。

■ In Hawthorne's famous novel, the scarlet letter is a **symbol** for adultery.

在霍桑知名的小說中，紅字是姦淫罪的**象徵**。

....

theme 主題

戲劇或小說的主要意義；中心思想。

■ Ambition and revenge are common **themes** in Shakespeare's plays.

在莎士比亞的劇作中，野心與報復是常見的**主題**。

....

tragedy 悲劇

嚴肅且有悲傷結局的戲劇。

■ *Macbeth*, the shortest of Shakespeare's plays, is a **tragedy**.

莎士比亞最短的劇作《馬克白》是部**悲劇**。

....